LONE SURVIVOR

(An Alex Hawkins Action Thriller —Book 1)

VIN STRONG

Vin Strong

Vin Strong is the author of the BRIANNA DAGGER spy thriller series, comprising five books (and counting), of the ZACK FORCE thriller series, comprising five books (and counting); and of the ALEX HAWKINS thriller series, comprising five books (and counting).

An avid reader and lifelong fan of the thriller genres, Vin loves to hear from you, so please feel free to visit vinstrongauthor.com to learn more and stay in touch.

ISBN: 978-1-0943-9786-3

BOOKS BY VIN STRONG

ZACK FORCE THRILLER SERIES
PATRIOT FORCE (Book #1)
PATRIOT DOWN (Book #2)
PATRIOT RISING (Book #3)
PATRIOT STRIKE (Book #4)
PATRIOT TARGET (Book #5)

BRIANNA DAGGER THRILLER SERIES
MAZE OF SPIES (Book #1)
MAZE OF TRAITORS (Book #2)
MAZE OF LIES (Book #3)
MAZE OF SHADOWS (Book #4)
MAZE OF SECRETS (Book #5)

ALEX HAWKINS THRILLER SERIES
LONE SURVIVOR (Book #1)
LONE TARGET (Book #2)
LONE WOLF (Book #3)
LONE COMMAND (Book #4)
LONE STRIKE (Book #5)

PROLOGUE

Mahmoud carefully straightened his tie and examined his face in the mirror. It looked soft and boyish without his beard. He would be very grateful to grow that back.

"Flight 237 nonstop to Dubai now boarding Captains Club members, military veterans and first responders."

Mahmoud brushed a fleck of dust from his lapel and grabbed his briefcase. He smiled at a young boy who eagerly showed him the toy airplane he was carrying. The woman's mother smiled gratefully at him for showing her son attention.

I'm sure many men show your son attention so they can stare at your bare shoulders and midriff, he thought. *And your ankles and bare feet. I'm sure you love every second of it.*

He forced his distaste away. This wasn't a *jihad*. This was just business. The Americans' sin would take care of itself, or else Allah would bring judgment to them in His time.

"Flight 237 nonstop to Dubai now boarding First Class passengers."

He took a seat and waited for his group to be called. Yusef passed him and showed his boarding pass to the gate agent. The two men didn't look at each other.

Besides Yusef, there were five others. Abdul would handle business class. Amal, Bashir and Hasam would stay with him in coach. Cyrus was in the first row of first class. He would handle the cockpit. Seven men to hijack an airplane that carried almost three hundred passengers.

He resisted the urge to check his briefcase. The weapon was still there, and nothing had happened since this morning that could have broken it. He needed to have faith. This was not a *jihad*, but he was still faithful, and Allah would bless his business. He was sure of it.

"Flight 237 nonstop to Dubai now boarding Business class passengers."

"Bye! Have a safe flight!"

Mahmoud turned around and saw the young boy from earlier waving eagerly at him as he held his harlot mother's hand.

"We're going to Disneyworld!" the boy proudly announced.

"Oh yeah? I'm going to Dubai. That's like Disneyworld for adults?"

The boy's eyes widened. "Is that in Florida too?"

Mahmoud laughed, as did the whore.

"Dubai's far away from Florida, buddy," the woman said, smiling down at her son, then lifting a shy, slightly desperate gaze to Mahmoud.

She was attracted to him. Many women were attracted to Mahmoud. American women for some reason preferred him without his beard. Many of them were desperate like this woman here. Perhaps that was why they dressed in bed clothes when they were out in public.

He kept his smile and said, "Dubai *is* far away. It's all the way across the ocean."

The boy's eyes were the size of dinner plates now. The idea of something existing across the ocean was unfathomable to him. "Across the *ocean?*"

"All the way across. It's in a country called the United Arab Emirates." *Known to the faithful as the pimple on Saudi Arabia's back.*

"United Airb Demirus?"

The woman laughed again. "Close enough, bud."

"Flight 6755 to Orlando now boarding groups one and two."

"That's us, buddy," the mother said. "Come on. We need to get going." She looked up at Mahmoud and smiled. "Have a safe flight."

"You too. Your son is adorable."

She flushed red, as though he had just told her that she was adorable. "Thank you. He's a charmer, for sure."

He watched them walk away for a few seconds to satisfy the American requirement for politeness, then turned ahead.

"Flight 237 nonstop to Dubai now boarding Group One."

He stood and picked up his briefcase, then walked toward the gate. An old white man with a beer gut wearing a tan fisherman's jacket over a gray t-shirt and a pair of cargo shorts stood in front of him. When the gate agent scanned his boarding pass, he turned to Mahmoud and said, "In God's hands now."

Mahmoud smiled. "Yes, it is." He lifted his pass to the gate agent and smiled at her. She flushed a little but did a better job of hiding her interest than the unwed mother.

"Say," the old man said. "You look spiffy. You sure you're not supposed to be in business class?"

"Too expensive," Mahmoud said. "I spent all of my money on the suit."

The old man seemed to feel this was the funniest thing anyone had said in history. He was still laughing when they reached the aircraft.

"What seat are you in?" he asked Mahmoud.

"15G," Mahmoud replied. *Please Allah, don't let him be seated next to me.*

"Ah, well. I'm 30B. I paid extra for early boarding."

Thank Allah. "I'll let you go ahead of me then. You have farther to walk."

"Thank you, young man. Enjoy your flight."

"You as well, sir."

Mahmoud carefully maneuvered his briefcase past the smiling flight attendants and disinterested first class passengers. Amal had leaned his chair back and closed his eyes. He would pretend to nap until the time came to take the plane. Mahmoud wished he could have it so easy, but he was not a convincing false sleeper. Abdul had his laptop open already and was going through the motions of purchasing a plot of land from somewhere named Visalia. He also didn't look up as Mahmoud passed.

Mahmoud reached his seat and carefully placed his briefcase into the overhead compartment. He felt a rush of anxiety watching it leave his hand, but it was important. If he carried it with him, it could look suspicious. They didn't know where the Air Marshal on this flight was, but it was best to assume that everyone viewed them with suspicion. He would retrieve it when the time came.

He took his seat, an aisle seat to make it easier for him to move when he needed. That meant he needed to get up twice when his seatmates arrived, but that was all right. He was pleased to see that his seatmates were a Bengali couple. The woman wore a hijab, and though she wore pants, they were loose-fitting and offered nothing to titillate him. More importantly, she kept her eyes lowered and allowed her husband to speak for them when they greeted him.

He felt sorry for them. Perhaps he could speak to Yusef and ensure that they were treated well.

He buckled in, took a deep breath and settled in for his flight. If all went well, he would leave this flight a very rich man.

CHAPTER ONE

Three hours earlier

"Echo Base, this is Echo One! We are going down! Repeat, we are going down! Mayday, mayday, over!"

The Sikorsky Blackhawk helicopter shuddered and dipped as the pilot struggled to minimize the effect of having their tail rotor shot off. He was a good pilot and doing as well as anyone could in this situation, but the helicopter was unsavable. They were going down, and they were going down hard.

"Brace for impact, boys!" Lieutenant Commander Alex Hawkins called. "We're gonna have a fun landing!"

"Hell yeah!" Chief Petty Officer Jackson echoed. "Time to play, boys!"

Jackson met Alex's eyes, the knowledge in his own evident. No one was going to make it out alive.

Twelve years in the Navy, and I'm going to die in a fucking helicopter crash, *Alex thought.* What a shitty way to go.

The other members of the team braced and shared equally grim looks with each other. They knew they weren't going to make it, but they were United States Navy SEALs, and they would be damned if they died cowards.

Jackson clapped his hand on Alex's shoulder and nodded to him. Alex nodded back.

They braced for impact and listened as the increasingly panicked pilot narrated their deaths to command.

"Echo Base, this is Echo One! Altitude five hundred feet and falling fast! We're going to hit hard! Four hundred. Oh shit… Three hundred! Echo Base, we are going to crash! Repeat, this will be a crash landing!"

The pilot managed to keep something resembling composure until they reached one hundred feet. Then he just repeated, "Oh fuck oh fuck oh fuck oh fuck oh FUCK!"

***

Alex's eyes opened. He reached over and tapped the button on his alarm clock. The ringing ceased, and he rolled out of bed, instantly alert as always. Of all the skills he had retained from his time in the military, the ability to fall asleep instantly and wake to full alertness instantly was probably the most valuable. He checked his phone. No new messages. He was still assigned to Flight 237. It was rare that Pat changed things up on him the morning of a flight, but it had happened before.

He headed downstairs and started coffee and breakfast. Eggs, Bacon, country potatoes and a fruit bowl with blackberries, blueberries, strawberries and bananas. Conventional wisdom said to eat light before a flight, but Alex never got motion sickness.

As he sipped his coffee, he went over the flight briefing again. Nonstop to Dubai, depart at nine-twenty-five am arrive six-fifteen am. Adventure Airlines Flight 237, Boeing 787-9. Two hundred eighty-eight passengers, eleven cabin crew including chef, four flight crew including two relief crew. Pretty typical stuff.

The airline was new though. Well, the airline itself wasn't new, but this was the first time it would be flying to Dubai. Most nonstops from the U.S. to the resort destination went through Emirates and used the massive Airbus A380. The 787 wasn't a small airplane by any means, but it was considerably smaller than the big Airbus. Adventure was hoping to offer a value package that made Dubai accessible to people who were only sort-of rich.

Not that he cared much about Adventure Airline's business strategy. The only reason this mattered to him was because security on new flights tended to be more stringent but less effective. They would be strictly by-the-book, and their focus would be on checking every item off of a list rather than ensuring the flight was actually safe. He and his partner would have to be on high alert.

The job of Air Marshal was probably one of the most overlooked jobs in the country. Even after the events of September eleventh, 2001, few people thought of Air Marshals, despite the fact that the successful performance of their job was what ensured there wouldn't be a repeat of that disaster. Air Marshals protected flights departing from and returning to the United States from threats such as hijackers, bombers and other terrorists.

Fortunately, most of the time they rarely had to deal with threats more significant than unruly passengers who had a little too much to

5

drink and needed to be restrained. Even more fortunately, those minor occurrences were also rare.

But that didn't mean they could relax. The consequences of allowing even a minor threat to go unaddressed at forty thousand feet could be disastrous. It was his job to ensure those threats were addressed. It was his partner's job to coordinate things from the ground and ensure that any resources he needed were provided to him as swiftly as possible.

He wondered sometimes why he'd chosen to be an Air Marshal. After losing his team in that crash, he half-expected to be turned off of flying for the rest of his life. Of course, flying in an air-conditioned jetliner over civilian airways was a bit different than flying in a military helicopter in a combat zone. Maybe he just gravitated to what he knew.

Or maybe protecting people in the air was his way of making amends.

His phone buzzed. His partner, Sarah Castillo. *On my way.*

He replied. *See you there.*

Sarah was driving from Mahwah, New Jersey, forty miles away. Even in the comparatively light traffic of Sunday morning, it would take her over an hour to reach the airport. He would reach the airport around the same time even though he would be leaving thirty minutes later.

He finished his breakfast and headed upstairs to the shower. Another skill he had retained from the SEALs was the ability to brush his teeth, shower thoroughly and dress completely in under fifteen minutes. Twenty minutes after he stepped into the shower, he was in his car headed to John F. Kennedy International Airport.

Traffic was beginning to wake up, and Alex smiled a little. "Light" traffic didn't mean the same thing in New York City as it did in Des Moines. Five-thirty on a Sunday morning, and the roads were already busy.

His smile faded as he thought of Des Moines. Ben still lived there. He would probably live there his entire life. Ben was a year younger than Alex, but in a lot of ways, he had inherited the Hawkins birthright. He had the mind for business that Alex never had and was the natural choice to inherit the company their great-grandfather had founded over a century ago. While Alex was serious and reserved, like their mother, Ben took after their father and had a gregarious personality that had landed him the position of Chairman of the Board of Hawkins Oil at twenty-one years of age despite a push by their late father's partners to divest shares among the surviving partners.

Had a gregarious personality, anyway. It had been quite some time since that side of him had shown, if it even existed anymore. Ben was now, if anything, even more serious than Alex, and had earned a reputation for ruthlessness.

The two brothers had at one time been close as… well, as brothers, but a rift had grown between them. It started when Alex chose to pursue a career in the military rather than join Ben at the helm of the family business. Ben was the natural choice to lead the business, and Alex didn't begrudge him their father's favor in that regard. Still, the family assumed that he would take some sort of role with the company. The reaction when Alex instead chose to join the Navy was rather unsupportive.

"The Navy? What the hell are you going to do in the Navy?"

"I imagine I'll protect and serve."

The younger Hawkins brother scoffed. "That's the police department, dumbass. You're going to be sailing the ocean blue. Have you ever even been on a boat?"

"There's a first time for everything."

Ben rolled his sky-blue eyes and shook his head. The fine blonde hair that hung in soft curls on top of his movie-star features reminded Alex of their mother. Everything else about Ben reminded him of their father. How odd that Alex took after their father in looks and their mother in personality while Ben was the precise opposite of him.

"You're trading a tenth-floor office with your own private bathroom and a secretary who looks like she was disqualified for Miss Universe for being too pretty for a bunk underneath a smelly man and a latrine shared with thirty other smelly men. You realize this, right?"

Alex chuckled. "I wouldn't go sleeping with your secretaries, Ben."

"Literal as always. I'm talking about you, Alex. You're literally giving up on a dream that most people will never get to experience."

Alex chuckled again. "Come on, Ben. You and I both know I'd end up shuffled to some meaningless mid-level position with no authority and kept as far from the business's operations as possible. You're the businessman, not me."

"I'm also your brother. You'd be riding my coattails. You'd get a meaningless upper-level position with no authority and kept as far from the business's operations as possible. And you'd get a private office and a woman who looks like she walked out of your dreams to fulfill every single one of them in real life."

Alex shook his head. "Not for me, man."

Ben's smile faded a little. "Not even for me? We said we'd be partners forever. Remember that?"

"We were kids, Ben."

"We're still kids."

"I'm not. And you won't be next year."

"So you're eighteen now, and suddenly you're an old, wise man?" Ben's smile was completely gone now. "I don't give a shit if you know how to read a balance sheet. You're my brother, and I love you. I don't want you getting shot in some jungle when you and I could be toasting our health and fabulous wealth every weekend while watching the Chiefs get steamrolled by literally every other team in the NFL."

"I don't plan on getting shot. Besides, I'm joining the Navy. More likely than not, I'll be cleaning a latrine shared by thirty smelly men, not running through the jungle with a rifle strapped to my back."

Ben sighed. He looked away from Alex for a moment, and Alex felt a touch of guilt.

"Hey. You're still my brother, man. We'll still be toasting our health and fabulous wealth. I'll just be doing it in a uniform, and you'll be doing it in a twenty-thousand-dollar Italian suit."

The ghost of a smile returned to Ben's lips. "All right." He turned back to Alex. "I guess I'm proud of you."

Alex grinned. "I'm proud of you too. Have fun with your secretaries."

Ben shook his head. "Nope. Amanda's the only woman for me."

"You're seventeen. You're going to meet lots of women."

"You got a problem with Amanda?"

"Not at all. I'm just saying keep your horizons open."

"Says the guy who just signed all of his horizons over to the United States Government."

Alex laughed again. "Fair point, brother."

The sky began to lighten as dawn approached. Traffic had slowed to a stroll now. In another hour or so, it would slow to a crawl, although again, that was relative. If the cars were moving, it didn't count as traffic for New York. Alex didn't need to check the time, but he did it anyway. Six-ten. He would reach the airport in five minutes.

As he followed the signs for employee parking, he went through a mental checklist. He didn't need to do this any more than he needed to check his clock to know the time, but once more, he did it anyway.

Step one: park the car in the section reserved for Air Marshals. Air Marshals were supposed to travel incognito, but despite Alex's repeated suggestions, they still used reserved parking spaces and a private security entrance at most airports. Convenience mattered more to most of his colleagues than concealment.

Step two: check in at the private security entrance. There he would inform airport authorities about his flight and seating assignment and receive his boarding pass. The pass would be for a seat in economy, but it would identify him as eligible for pre-boarding due to his military service. It was technically public knowledge that he was former US Navy, and his ID was a VA one, so he wasn't really losing any stealth for that.

Step three: rendezvous with Sarah. She would be at the TSA offices and brief him on the flight. That wasn't necessary, but it was protocol, and both he and Sarah agreed that protocol was important to the performance of their jobs.

Step four: board the aircraft. Once on board, his job would officially begin. The TSA would have already swept the craft for anything dangerous as well as screened the passengers and baggage. With the current state of technology, it was very difficult to sneak any form of contraband onboard a flight, but he was there for those rare occasions when it happened anyway.

Not that he was concerned. In four years with the Air Marshals, he had flown one hundred fifteen times. Seven times, he had needed to subdue an unruly passenger who drank too much and either panicked or became belligerent. The other one hundred eight flights had proceeded without incident.

Still, he was always prepared. That was another skill he had retained from the SEALs. As Old Joe Lincoln used to say, "Shit happens when you're not looking."

Shit never happened to Alex.

He showed his ID to the gate guard at the employee parking lot and was waved through. He took a deep breath and released it in a heavy sigh.

He allowed himself one final wistful thought of Ben, then pushed everything from his mind but his job.

CHAPTER TWO

John F. Kennedy was the busiest airport in New York, but surprisingly only the sixth busiest in the United States and the fourteenth busiest worldwide. It was also Sunday, so while the airport certainly wasn't empty, it was far from as crowded as it would be during the work week. That was another oddity. Even in the heyday of the information age, business travel still accounted for far more air traffic than tourism.

Dubai airport would be significantly busier. Though known mostly for tourism, Dubai was a major hub for international business as well, and since they would be arriving Monday morning, the airport and the city itself would be packed. Far more well-managed than JFK, though. It was easy to make things seamless when you could afford to spend billions per year on public transportation and security.

Alex made his way to the TSA offices. This was another frustration of his. If he was going to enter through an employee entrance and take a separate security check, then he should at least be able to reach the TSA offices without walking in full view of other passengers.

If he was questioned about walking into the office, he would just say he needed to reapply for expedited security clearance, not uncommon for businesspeople to do, though it wasn't exactly common for people to apply for expedited security clearance and then travel economy.

No one questioned him, though. It was less than thirty years since terrorists had flown airplanes into the World Trade Center and the Pentagon, but people forgot so easily.

He walked into the office and identified himself to the receptionist. The receptionist looked to be about twenty years old and really should shave a few more years before trying to grow out a beard. He looked wide-eyed at Alex, as though seeing an Air Marshal was the coolest thing possible. He must be new.

"Yes, sir, um… I think… your boss is in the other room?"

"My partner. And which room is that?"

"Oh. Partner. Sorry. Um, looks like meeting room A."

Alex smiled at him. "Thank you."

The young man blushed, and it occurred to Alex that the wide-eyed stare and stammering speech might be prompted by something other than awe at his position. He allowed himself a moment to feel flattered, then refocused on his job.

Sarah waited for him in the room. As always, she nodded professionally and shook his hand.

Sarah Castillo was twenty-seven years old, twelve years younger than Alex, but with a year more experience with the Air Marshals since she applied straight after college rather than pursuing a career in the military first.

She was also beautiful. Five-foot-seven with long, flowing hair, deep-brown eyes, tanned skin and a figure that, as Ben would have said, would disqualify her from Miss Universe for being too pretty, she was known among the Marshals not just for her capability but for her attractiveness. One of Alex's favorite amusements was watching other Marshals try to impress her or gain her attention.

He wasn't interested himself. He and Sarah were partners, and the idea of romance between them was beyond out of the question. When hundreds, perhaps thousands, of lives depended on the performance of your duty, there was no room for personal relationships. They considered themselves friends, but that was as far as it would ever go.

Sarah felt the same way, and as soon as she realized Alex wasn't going to try to seduce her, she asked for and received him as a partner.

"How was the drive?" she asked, taking her seat again.

Alex shrugged. "It was a drive." He remained standing.

"It's okay for you to sit, soldier," she said with a smile. "I'm not your boss."

He returned her smile. "I feel like standing today."

She shrugged. "Suit yourself." She tapped a few keys on her laptop and said, "Okay, so: Adventure Airlines Flight 237, Boeing 787-9, two hundred eighty-eight passengers including yourself, eleven cabin crew, four flight crew. Aircraft scheduled to depart Terminal 4, Gate A5 at nine-twenty-five a.m, scheduled to arrive six-fifteen a.m. Dubai International Airport Terminal 3, Gate B15. No delays. This is the first flight to Dubai by Adventure Airlines, so it's the first flight to Dubai by this flight crew. Captain Jean Hollister, five years as captain, twenty-two with the airline. First Officer Jonathan Grant, also five years as first officer, six with the airline, eighteen years total as a commercial pilot."

"Eighteen? That's a long time to be a first officer."

"He started with a commuter airline and clawed his way up through the ranks. He's only forty, so he's got some time to make captain. Not that it matters, but Jean is forty-seven."

"Damn. You friend these guys on social media or something?"

She lifted her eyes to his. "I'm working with you. Frankly, I expected you to chastise me for not having their next of kin and medical information."

He chuckled. "No, this is great. Any flags?"

Flags referred to elevated threat factors. They could range from something as simple as a new cabin crew to something as dangerous as a bomb threat.

"First flight to destination by airline, first flight to destination by flight crew. Other than that, nothing."

"Got it. Nice, easy flight."

"Almost makes you wish someone would try something, right?"

"Hell no."

She laughed and said, "Just kidding. Okay, so the plane itself won't be ready for boarding for another two and a half hours. Want to grab some breakfast?"

"I ate already, but I'll watch you eat breakfast."

She grimaced. "That sounds weird."

"I'd rather not know why."

She chuckled again and said, "Well, I suppose since it's you, I'll put up with it. Come on. There's a new donut shop I want to try."

This time it was Alex's turn to grimace. "A donut? For breakfast?"

"They sell burritos too. Why? What do you have against donuts?"

"Nothing, but how do you stay in this kind of shape eating donuts all the time?"

"All the time? It's one donut, Alex. You know what? I want you to order a donut, and I want to see you eat it. You should allow some enjoyment into your life. And to answer your question, I work out every day. I'm also still young, unlike a certain grumpy old man who feels a need to question my dietary choices."

"All right, truce. I give up. Forget I said anything."

"Now he's moping again. I want you to drink some more coffee too."

She led them from the TSA offices toward the terminal's food court. After only five minutes, the terminal was already noticeably busier. This truly was the city that never slept.

The donut shop proudly announced that the sweet treats they baked fresh daily were vegan and free of gluten, allergens and chemicals.

They were one hundred percent organic and environmentally sustainable. The coffee was something called Rainforest Alliance certified.

"Are these actually donuts or donut-shaped granola bars?"

"Quiet. You gave me crap for wanting a donut, you don't get to have an opinion."

She ordered a green chile breakfast burrito, a maple bar and a light roast. Alex, under Sarah's watchful gaze, ordered a plain glazed ring and a cappuccino.

"A glazed ring donut? Could you get any blander?"

"I like the basics. My coffee's fancy."

"Oh yeah, a plain oat milk cappuccino. You're really branching out today."

"I'd order it with whole milk if they carried it."

"That's even worse."

They sat at a table a little removed from the other diners, although with terminal traffic picking up rapidly, that probably wouldn't be the case for long. While they waited for their order, Sarah broached a subject Alex hoped he could avoid.

"How was your date last night?" Sara grinned conspiratorially as she said it, clearly expecting to hear titillating details. She was going to be disappointed.

He sighed. "I canceled."

"You *canceled?* On my best friend."

"I thought I was your best friend."

"Don't be an asshole. Are you serious? I thought she didn't text me because she spent the night with you and was too busy getting screwed into oblivion to reply."

"Boy, I just love hearing you talk about me screwing someone into oblivion."

"You don't get to have attitude with me. You stood up my best friend."

"I didn't stand her up. I texted her that I wasn't going to be able to make it."

"Oh? And why not? Were they playing *The Guns of Navarone* on tv last night?"

"I'm not that old. I know how to stream movies."

"Stop avoiding the subject. What the fuck, *mijo?*"

Alex sighed. "Look, I told you to stop setting me up with people. I told you when you mentioned her that I wasn't looking to date."

"And I told you to stop living like a monk."

"I'm not a monk. If you're so desperate for me to get laid, let's go find a closet somewhere. I'll screw *you* into oblivion."

She gave him a hard stare to indicate that she was done joking. "I care about you, *mijo*. I don't like seeing you lonely."

Alex sighed again. "I'll meet someone in my own time. I can't force myself to feel things for people."

"You're still dancing around the subject. You're turning forty in six months. You're not an angsty teenager. You're choosing to avoid feeling anything for anyone because you're afraid of showing your vulnerable side."

"Was I supposed to cry on Yareli's shoulder last night?" he said irritably. "Look, I don't need to date to feel happy."

"So you're happy? Right now? Your life as it is, you're happy? You go home and smile in the mirror and think, 'Damn, I really love my life.'"

"I'm surviving," he replied. "That's enough for right now."

"No it *isn't, mijo*. You know it isn't. You're hiding because it's easy, but you know as well as I do that if you spend your life in a hole, that's where you'll end up buried."

He lifted his hands and let them drop. He wanted to say something angry, but he knew that it wouldn't help. She wasn't the type of person to back down when she knew she was right.

But he really wasn't in a place to share his life with anyone. Not yet.

"I still have nightmares, Sarah. I still have flashbacks. I still can't go to fireworks shows. I'm not going to make that someone else's problem. When I can move on from the war, I'll start dating."

"That's not how it works, *mijo*. And this isn't about the war, anyway. It's about your brother."

"And this conversation is now over," Alex said curtly. "Sorry about your friend. Next time, spare the girl the disappointment and don't set me up with them."

He stood and tossed his donut wrapper and cappuccino cup in the nearby trash can. "I'm going to head to the gate," he said. "I'll talk to you later."

Sarah didn't reply. She stood and tossed the remains of her own food, her lips pressed in a thin line. She was really upset at him this time, and it didn't help that he had cut her off and was now walking away.

But she would have to deal with it. He never asked her to meddle in his personal life. Their relationship was supposed to be professional.

Maybe he should think about pulling away from the friendship and being more strict with the definition of professional.

Even as he said that, he rejected it. He was angry, and that was affecting his judgment. He liked Sarah as a friend. He just didn't like when she would pressure him to date. They were fighting now, but that would change in two hours. Business was business, and nothing mattered more than keeping people safe.

He thought of Ben, not as he was when Alex went to the Naval Academy but as he was the last time Alex saw him at their mother's funeral five weeks ago. He didn't speak to Alex, but his cold stare said more than words ever could. That stare lingered in his mind as he took a seat and waited for his flight to board.

Sarah was right about that too. Alex couldn't let anyone get close to him because anyone who got close to him got hurt. Just like Ben.

CHAPTER THREE

Alex met the airplane crew in the crew lounge. Air Marshals were never revealed to the passengers, but they were always introduced to the crew in case the crew needed to alert them of an emergency.

Alex smiled and did his best to appear non-threatening, a difficult task for the six-foot-one, two-hundred-ten-pound former Navy SEAL.

"Alex Hawkins. It's a pleasure to meet all of you. I'll be protecting your flight today."

The primary flight crew of Captain Hollister and First Officer Grant nodded, slightly bored expressions on their faces. They were old hands and had flown with many Air Marshals over the years. "Pleased to meet you," Captain Hollister said.

The relief crew was a little greener than the primary crew, and the relief copilot—a short, dark-haired man of around thirty, asked nervously. "Is there a reason we should be worried?"

"None at all," Alex reassured him. "We've gone through the manifest and there's no reason to believe this won't be a completely uneventful flight. The most you'll have to worry about is listening to a canned speech from the CEO at the holiday party this year to commemorate the first Adventure Airlines flight to Dubai."

The fifteen people present laughed politely. Alex turned his attention to the cabin crew and catalogued information. Four men, one of them the chef. Seven women. Ages ranging from thirty to forty, except for one flight attendant who appeared to be in her late twenties.

He focused his attention on her. She fidgeted nervously and stood a few feet apart from the others. She offered him an anxious smile but only held eye contact for a second before looking away. He decided to probe for a little more information.

"Any first-timers here?" he asked. "First time with the airline, first time as part of an aircrew, first time flying?"

The nervous girl lifted her hand. "Um… first time with the airline. I used to work for JetExpress out of Denver. We did a lot of regional flights to smaller airports in the Plains. Um… first time international, though."

A few of the older flight attendants rolled their eyes. First-timers always made things annoying, asking questions they should know the answers to and acting skittish around the passengers. They understood that everyone had a first time, but why did it have to be on *their* flight?

Alex smiled at the newcomer. "Well, you're in good hands. I've flown with Adventure several times, and they've been nothing but helpful and professional. You'll be fine. Make sure you review emergency alert procedures with the head flight attendant if you haven't already."

"We have," a thin-faced woman quickly replied. "No need to go over them again."

Alex kept his smile but put a touch of authority into his voice. "I want everyone to be safe today. If your flight attendants need to ask you fifty times what the procedures are, you'll go over them."

The thin-faced woman frowned slightly but didn't argue. "Yes, sir."

"All right," Alex said. "I'll be sitting in 30C just behind the wing. Most of you know this, but I'm going to say it anyway: treat me like any other economy class passenger. No special privileges, not that I will ask. No breaking rules, not that I will break any. No showing me any extra attention and no staring at me and trying to figure out where my gun is."

There was more polite laughter at that statement, except from the newcomer, who laughed with a touch of anxiety. Alex looked at her again and noticed how utterly breathtaking she was. She was five-foot-five he guessed, five-foot-eight in the stiletto heels she wore. She had long reddish-blonde hair that hung straight to her shoulders before ending in loose curls. She had bright green eyes and a slender figure that looked angelic and delicate at the same time.

No, Alex was definitely not a monk.

But he *was* a professional. He was here to do a job, not make a friend.

"Okay, does anyone have any questions?"

"Um, yes," the new flight attendant asked. "When do you board? Do we let you on when we board?"

The other flight attendants sighed, but otherwise kept their opinions to themselves.

"Good question, Miss…"

"Emma. Emma Johnson."

"Good question, Miss Johnson. I board with the first group. In my case, it's military veterans. Usually, I'll be issued a pass that says I'm part of the airline's club or that I've paid for early boarding privileges, but since I'm a veteran, I usually board with just my VA ID."

"You're a veteran? Who did you serve with?"

The rest of the crew rolled their eyes. She was going to be one of *those*.

Alex smiled patiently. "US Navy. I would love to tell you more at another time, but I'm sure you all have work to do before the flight. I'll see you on board."

"See you later!" Emma said brightly.

The head flight attendant cast her a sour look. Emma met her eyes and tossed her hair flippantly before leaving to get her flight bag. Alex liked that. She wasn't completely delicate.

"Anything we should know about flying into Dubai?" Captain Hollister asked. "I think this will be a first for all of us."

"It's just like any other airport, except that there won't be any delays, mistakes or gate changes with no notice," Alex replied. "Their facilities are nicer, the food's better, and if you need to get anywhere in the city, you'll either be riding in a Maybach or a Lamborghini."

Hollister's eyes widened. "Damn. So it's paradise, in other words."

"Yep. One of the few resort destinations that actually lives up to its name."

"Forget about the Maybach," First Officer Grant said. "They handle the approach and taxi us to the gate without any drama, and I'll kiss their asses with a smile on my face."

Hollister grimaced. "Lovely turn of phrase, Jack."

"Don't tell me you won't do the same thing."

***

Alex watched as passengers filed onto the plane. He liked his seat near the midpoint of the plane because it allowed him to reach anywhere onboard quickly, but it also meant he couldn't see the business or first-class passengers board. Not more than a brief glimpse before they took their seats, at least.

Much could be gleaned from a brief glimpse, though. For example, he could tell that the demure Bengali woman with the headscarf was cheating on her husband from the way she recoiled slightly at his touch. He could tell the husband knew from the way he let that touch linger once he knew it repelled her. He could tell that the mother flying with her child was terrified that her child would misbehave from the forced smile she wore and the tight grip she kept on the hood of his sweater.

He could tell that the child would be as well-behaved as a lamb from the bright smile he wore and the eagerness with which he looked out of his window.

He could also tell that no one on this flight gave any indication of being a threat. That wasn't a surefire guarantee, but it was a very good sign. The closest he came to worrying about anyone was a pot-bellied man in his fifties who let his eyes linger on Emma a little too long. Provided he didn't drink, that would likely be a non-issue, but if he threw too many back, he might decide to try for more than a look. Alex hoped if that would be a problem, it would reveal itself later in the flight so he didn't have to deal with a restrained passenger for hours.

Overall, though, this looked to be a pretty mundane assignment. He checked his phone. Ten minutes before takeoff. He didn't have to put his technology into airplane mode like the rest of the passengers since his phone used a proprietary and secure signal, but it would be better if he didn't get caught talking when no one was supposed to be able to talk.

So, he called Sarah now. "Hey, asshole," she said.

His shoulders released tension he didn't realize he was carrying. If she was teasing him again, then she wasn't mad at him anymore.

"Hey yourself," he said cheerfully. "Just wanted to let you know we're about to take off."

"Yeah, I got you. No delays leaving or arriving. Considering this is JFK, I'm surprised. You'll hit some weather on the way, but nothing to worry about. Your passengers will get jumpy, though."

"Well, I'm glad that's not my problem."

"So, any cute flight attendants?"

He thought immediately of Emma. "I'm going to hang up now."

"Ooh, there is. What's her name?"

"Come on. This is a business trip."

That was his way of reminding her that they were working now.

"You're no fun." Dropping the teasing voice, she said, "Everything's good on my end. I'll keep the signal open in case you run into anything. I plan on staying awake and never more then six inches from my phone for the entire flight, as always."

"Sounds good. Thanks, Sarah."

"No problem." The wall of professionalism came down a little once more when she said, "Chin up, okay? I'm not *that* pissed at you."

He smiled. "Okay. Talk to you later."

"Yep. Bye."

She hung up, and he sighed and settled in for his flight.

Another flight attendant—one of the men—stood up and began demonstrating emergency safety procedures. As usual, the airplane pulled smoothly away from the gate while the passengers' attention was directed toward the attendant or else toward the screens in front of their seat. People were less likely to panic and try to leave if the plane was already away from the gate. The only thing more terrifying than a plane crash was embarrassing yourself publicly, for example, making an entire airplane turn around because you suddenly realized you were afraid of heights.

The demonstration ended and the jet engines spooled up as Hollister ran through the last of her preflight checks. The passenger next to Alex, a middle-aged man in an outfit that only a retired person would wear, smiled at him. "Houston, all systems go."

Alex smiled politely but declined to respond. He did his job better when he wasn't distracted by conversation.

The plane started for the runway, and the passengers began murmuring to each other, some nervously, most excitedly. Dubai was a dream come true for many of them, and they talked eagerly of white sand beaches, world-class food, luxury cars, even more luxurious hotels and the slim but ever-present possibility of a vacation fling with an exotic individual with no inhibitions.

A few passengers gripped their armrests and closed their eyes, but fewer than on many flights. Alex didn't think there would be a panic this time around.

Then again, when they hit the weather, it might throw everything on its head. People who weren't experienced with flying thought that planes glided through the air like skates over ice. Most people didn't take well to the revelation that air could be just as choppy as water.

They reached the runway. The engines spooled up, rising from a hum to a roar. Hollister released the brakes, and the airplane launched forward.

Alex smiled when he saw the young boy from earlier, his face pressed against the window, his eyes wide with delight.

Enjoy the flight, kid.

CHAPTER FOUR

"Okay, folks, the captain has just turned off the seatbelt sign. You are now free to move about the cabin. At this time, we would like to remind you that this flight is entirely non-smoking. This includes all locations in the passenger cabin as well as lavatories. Thank you and have a safe flight."

The passenger next to Alex leaned over and said in a voice that wasn't nearly as quiet as he thought it was, "I remember on my first flight back in 1987, they handed me a complementary cigarette. The flight attendant even lit it for me. Pretty young thing, curly red hair, gorgeous green eyes, best smile you've ever seen. I would have given anything for a moment alone with her, but I knew better than to ask. Even back then, they didn't like it when passengers harassed the girls."

"Oh yeah?" Alex said noncommittally. "Got it."

"Matter of fact, now that I remember it, some poor fellow did try to ask her for a favor. He ended up sitting next to the Air Marshal for the entire flight, hands folded in his lap just like in Sunday School." The man laughed. "Poor kid. Even the flight attendant felt bad for him. Gave him her number just to cheer him up. Don't know if he ever called her though. If that had been me, I don't think I'd ever fly again."

An annoyed passenger glanced the older man's way, and he quieted. He rolled his eyes at Alex as though he couldn't believe the nerve of some people to interrupt his story like that, then said in a slightly quieter but still very quiet voice, "Guess I'll watch the movie. Don't want to piss anyone off."

"Sounds good."

Alex looked around the cabin. The anxious passengers had relaxed enough to open their eyes, but they still looked like they wished they could go anywhere else than where they were. The other passengers exhibited the usual mix of eager and bored. About half were enjoying the in-flight entertainment. The rest either read books or played games on their phones, except for a few who slept.

The flight attendants busied themselves preparing for service. Alex focused on Emma, who was checking the cart for the rear half of the economy passengers. She noticed him looking and smiled, flushing a little. He returned his smile and forced himself to look away.

You're not here for that, he reminded himself.

He ordered a mineral water and a fruit cup for his snack. When Emma placed the water on his tray, he was keenly aware of the scent of coconut and almond in her hair. Damn it, what was the matter with him? He saw beautiful women every day. Why was this one so different?

He was grateful when she moved on, and he could turn his attention back to his job. His phone buzzed, a text from Sarah.

Weather's moved on. Smooth sailing from here to Dubai.

He texted back, *Good to know. Thank you.*

On cue, Captain Hollister's voice came over the PA. "Folks, it looks like that storm cell has moved north, so we should expect minimal turbulence for the remainder of the flight. Please keep in mind that there is *no* smoking on this flight. We had an incident on our last flight where a gentleman thought the rules didn't apply to him and the entire plane—passengers and all—had to wait for two hours before reaching the gate so that the airplane's plumbing could be flushed. For the sake of all of us, please don't be that guy or gal."

A whiff of coconut and almond caught Alex's nose again, and Emma passed a moment later. Her hips swayed gently as she pushed the cart back toward the galley, and Alex sighed. In hindsight, he should have gone on that date with Yareli after all. He would have been able to focus better if he had gotten this out of his system.

His mind drifted back to the first and so far only relationship he'd had.

Hannah clamped a hand over his mouth and Alex quieted. The two of them stilled and listened as the patrol passed overhead.

"What are we even doing here, anyway?" an irritated voice asked. That would be Petty Officer Third Class Hooper. "The Taliban hasn't launched a missile at a US vessel in almost a year."

"That's because we're here to make sure it doesn't happen." Petty Officer First Class Dowser replied.

"They could at least let us go ashore," Hooper complained.

"You think you're getting laid in Afghanistan, Hooper? You can't even catch tail when we're home."

"You never know until you try."

Alex and Hannah met each other's eyes and laughed. The two of them had been 'catching tail' almost nonstop since meeting each other three weeks ago when they arrived for deployment on the USS Dakota.

They waited until they couldn't hear the patrol again. Then Hannah pulled her hand from Alex's mouth and replaced it with her lips, and the two of them finished what they had started.

Alex smiled wistfully. He and Hannah had dated for the entirety of that deployment. He wasn't even sure if you could call it dating while you were on deployment. They barely had time to sneak off and enjoy themselves. There were no actual dates, just moments of relief from months at sea. They planned to keep seeing each other when they returned home, but once they did, they realized that they didn't have as much in common as they thought they did and ended up parting amicably.

The sea would do that to you. It was like being drunk. When your options were limited, you took what you could get.

That was his first deployment. His next one was on the USS Abraham Lincoln, and while he'd had a few anonymous encounters on the city-sized ship, he hadn't ever seen anyone more than twice. When he returned from that deployment, he was promoted to Lieutenant Junior Grade and selected for BUD/s. After that, there was no such thing as screwing around, in any sense of the word. He was a SEAL, and his life, his love, his lady was the Team.

He'd always thought he would find a woman and settle down when he left the SEALs, but after his brother was hurt, the part of him that could accept happiness had shattered. Another thing Sarah was right about. He carried a lot of guilt from his time in the military, but he was ruined long before he lost his team over Afghanistan.

The airplane bounced slightly as it hit an air pocket. The passengers froze as one and looked around at each other. Alex smiled a little. *Nothing to worry about, folks. We're all—*

Before he could finish that thought, the plane lurched suddenly to the left. Then it dropped sickeningly. Alex frowned and immediately scanned the aircraft for threats.

The plane lurched again, and passengers began to scream. The cabin tilted to the right, and then the plane dropped once more. Alex heard a whine as the plane picked up speed and air screamed against the flight control surfaces.

He bounced up and down in his chair as the cabin shook like a child shaking a rattle. The passengers cried out, and several grabbed their armrests and closed their eyes. A couple of them vomited. One of them didn't manage to grab a sick bag first, and an acrid, sour smell began to permeate the cabin. The flight attendants looked nervously at each other, and the head flight attendant picked up the phone and called the cockpit.

The airplane lurched final time, then Alex felt his chair push into him as the nose swung up. Then it leveled out and just as soon as it had started, the turbulence stopped.

The passengers sat in silence for over a minute. Then one of them laughed nervously. More laughter joined the first, and slowly, people began to relax.

Most of them anyway. A few still shook with fright and several of them shouted for flight attendants and asked, "What's going on? What's happening?"

The little boy who had been so excited to fly earlier was now crying. His mother tried to console him, but her own face was white as a sheet. Alex watched as Emma knelt in front of him and tried to reassure him that everything was going to be okay. It was just a little bit of turbulence and totally normal.

Except that wasn't normal. That kind of turbulence only occurred if they flew into a thunderstorm, and Sarah told him the storm had moved on.

He texted her. *Just went through crazy turbulence. Did we hit weather after all?*

The reply she sent did nothing to reassure him. *Negative. Clear and smooth as a pane of glass. How bad was the turbulence?*

He frowned. *Bad. Thought we flew through a hurricane.*

A moment later, she replied. *Not the weather. Not sure what's going on, but worth looking into.*

His frown deepened. If there wasn't any weather, then the plane had malfunctioned somehow. That could be a coincidence, or it could be sabotage.

Hollister's voice came over the PA again. "Uh, folks, this is Captain Hollister. Looks like we might have hit some rough air after all. My instruments are showing clear weather from here on out, so that should be a one-time thing. For the time being, though, I'm going to put the seatbelt light on. If you can all hang tight, thank you."

Alex looked around at the nervous aircrew and frightened passengers.

Mostly frightened passengers. One of the passengers near the front of the cabin in the premium economy seats looked over his shoulder with a look of smug satisfaction.

That didn't necessarily mean anything suspicious. If he was an experienced traveler, then he had likely encountered this kind of turbulence before and found it a little amusing that everyone was freaking out over it.

Still, it was Alex's job to investigate anything suspicious. He texted Sarah. *Can you get flight details?*

Got them. The plane's navigation system sent an alarm ping to the satellite three minutes ago. The system rebooted forty-five seconds later. That probably explains your turbulence.

Good to know. Now I need a full bio on seat 12C.

One moment.

Alex looked back at the passenger while he waited for Sarah to call him back. He was still smiling softly as the cabin crew gradually worked to calm the passengers. His eyes didn't hold mirth, though. Something else was behind that gaze. It looked to Alex more like eagerness.

For what?

His phone buzzed.

Rajput Bashir, 41. 5'9" 160 pounds. No criminal history. BA in computer science from the University of Miami. MA in software engineering UC Berkeley. Seven years with Aleph Computing. Now he works for an IT firm as a customer support specialist

It was off for someone to choose a career in customer service instead of a six- or possibly seven-figure job as a software developer.

Then again, Alex had chosen a career in the Navy over a seven- or possibly eight-figure position with his brother's company. It wasn't suspicious in and of itself.

But that smile…

Alex decided he would have to keep an eye on Bashir. Something fishy was going on.

CHAPTER FIVE

"What the hell was that?" the passenger next to Alex asked. "Think that was a hurricane? There's clear skies, though."

"I don't know," Alex said.

"Scared the bejeezus out of me. I don't scare easily, but that was insane. Felt like we were going to crash. You ever been in a plane crash?"

"Echo Base, this is Echo one! We are going down! Repeat, we are going down!"

"No. Can't say that I have."

"Me either. I'd like to keep it that way. Hey! Miss!"

One of the flight attendants—not Emma—cast an annoyed look at him before plastering on a fake smile. She walked over and said, "Sir, I assure you that the flight crew has everything under control. We experienced a bit of mild turbulence, and now—"

"*Mild* turbulence? The whole damned airplane shook like a can of sardines!"

"Sir, I need you to keep your voice down. There is nothing to worry about."

The man frowned, but he lowered his voice. "I just want to know what happened. The captain said clear skies."

"The skies were clear, but air pockets can form even in clear skies. There's nothing to be afraid of. I know it seemed frightening, but the entire episode was over in less than a minute, and as you can see, the flight crew has everything under control now."

The man glowered, but he nodded and said, "All right. As long as you say we're safe." He smiled. A little nervously. "I'm trusting you, Amanda."

Amanda smiled again, relieved that the boisterous older man wasn't going to be a problem after all. "I promise you everything is perfectly fine."

She looked at Alex, who shook his head slightly. She nodded professionally and left without doing anything that could reveal his cover.

"You think she's telling the truth?" the older man asked.

Alex nodded. "I've flown many times before. That kind of turbulence isn't common, but it's nothing to worry about either. We're fine."

He nodded and said, "Well, I'm going to finish my movie then. Let me know if anything else happens, will ya?"

Alex nodded, and the old man put his earphones back in.

Alex looked toward the front of the cabin again at Bashir. He was smiling and talking to a female passenger in her thirties who appeared attracted to the older but well put-together Bashir. What was it about flying that made everyone horny?

It was probably just anxiety over the turbulence. Most people didn't know how to deal with anxiety. That woman was probably just hoping that a little harmless flirtation would give her something to focus on other than the momentary episode of terror they had experienced.

"Next time I'm flying Emirates," a voice from across the aisle said. "They have those big A380s, the superjumbos. Those things don't jerk around the way these smaller planes do."

Tell me you don't understand flying without telling me you don't understand flying, Alex thought drily. While it was true to a point that larger aircraft didn't feel turbulence as much, an air pocket as serious as the last one they had flown through would have shaken even one of the mammoth double-decker Airbuses.

If they had flown through an air pocket. The navigation system had blinked out at the same time, but that shouldn't have affected the airplane's trim. That suggested that it *was* an air pocket, but the timing was too close to be coincidental.

But what could have sabotaged the plane for forty-five seconds? And why? It didn't make sense for someone to do that. All signs pointed to nothing to worry about.

But Alex was worried anyway.

His phone buzzed. Sarah.

Getting some telemetry data from the black box. Weird energy spikes right around the time the navigation system went down. Not sure yet if it affected other aircraft systems. I'll keep you posted. Anything suspicious from Bashir?

Alex looked back toward the front of the economy cabin. Bashir was talking to another passenger, this one an elderly male. He was smiling gently at the old man and nodding his head reassuringly. Alex couldn't tell what he was saying, but he was clearly trying to comfort the old man.

Alex relaxed a little. There was probably nothing to worry about. He texted Sarah back. *Nothing. He's calming some of the more anxious passengers. Probably just lapsed into momentary smugness when everyone was freaking out over the turbulence.*

Sounds like a smarmy little prick. At least he got his act together. I'll look through the manifest again just in case and see if we missed anything.

Thank you.

A minute later, his phone buzzed again. *Hey, at least the flight wasn't boring.*

He rolled his eyes and sent her a middle finger emoji. She replied with a laughing emoji, and Alex relaxed further.

The flight continued normally for the next two hours. People gradually calmed. The man sitting next to Alex finished his movie and started another. The nervous passengers had managed to calm themselves to the point where they could open their eyes and talk to others. The vomit had been cleaned up, and thanks to a few discreet sprays of air freshener from the attendants, the cabin didn't smell like the back of a dive bar anymore.

The little boy was asleep, cherubic face resting in open-mouthed relaxation as he leaned on his mother's lap. The mother smiled the special smile that only mothers wore and softly stroked his hair.

"You want kids?"

Alex looked at Hannah in horror, and she burst into laughter. "Your face! Oh my God. Not with me, *idiot. I mean, in general. Like ever."*

"Oh." He reddened and shrugged. "I don't know. Maybe. I haven't really thought about it."

"I want kids."

"Yeah?" He tried his best to appear interested, but he still felt a little nervous with the conversation. He liked Hannah, but they really weren't doing anything serious. They were just having a little fun. He didn't think of them as long-term. He didn't think she did either, but it was weird that they were talking about kids. Especially since they were both still so young. He was twenty-three, and Hannah was twenty-four.

"Yeah. Not a bunch, just like one or two. I don't know. I think I'd be a good mom."

"I think you'd be a great mom."

She rolled her eyes at him the way she always did when he complimented her. She couldn't seem to believe he would say anything nice about her for any reason other than to get in her pants. That was strange to Alex, since getting into her pants had never been difficult.

"Thanks," she said drily. "I think you'd be a terrible father."

"Hey!"

"Just kidding! God, why are you so sensitive today? Commander Gleason bust your balls again?"

"As a matter of fact, he said my team was the most organized he'd seen."

"Did he? Aww, that's so sweet. Good for you."

His eyes narrowed playfully. "You've got a bit of an attitude problem, Petty Officer."

She smiled coyly at him. "Yeah? Are you going to discipline me, Ensign Hawkins?"

"Sir?"

Alex looked up to see Emma looking down at him. Her smile took his breath away, and it was a half-second before he said, "Yes?"

"I was just wondering what your order for lunch was."

"Oh. Yes. I'll take the protein box, please."

"And to drink?"

"Just water."

"Sparkling, mineral or still?"

"Mineral, please."

She smiled again. "Thank you. And for you…"

Her voice trailed off when a snore came from Alex's traveling companion. She looked back at Alex and giggled a little. "If he wakes up, just tell him to press the call button, and we'll take his order."

"I'll do that. Thank you."

She headed to the row behind him, and he resisted the urge to turn around and let his eyes linger. On a whim, he texted Sarah. *You put me in the wrong mood this morning talking about dating.*

Does this mean you need more coffee or does this mean there's a pretty flight attendant who's making you rethink your vow of celibacy?

He hesitated before replying. He was setting himself up for a barrage of teasing that would probably last the rest of his career.

But there was almost no chance he would see Emma again after this flight. Flight Attendants were rotated just like Air Marshals. Both of them would almost certainly end up on different flights home.

The second part.

Details! Now!

He laughed.

Your age, blonde, green-eyed, great smile. Looks kind of like that Irish actress who played opposite John Wayne in that movie about the boxer, but more blonde than red in her hair.

Ooh, que rico. *I call the best man at the wedding.*

He laughed. *Nah, I'm working. Look, but no touch.*

Bullshit. Your job ends when the plane touches down. I expect a phone number and a first date scheduled, or I'll have Yareli waiting at your home when you get back.

Leave Yareli alone, for God's sake. And relax. I just said she's pretty. If you hadn't reminded me of how long it's been, I wouldn't even be thinking about this. I wasn't inviting you to cheer me on, I was complaining that you've made it hard for me to focus on my job.

She didn't respond for several minutes, and Alex wondered if he'd gone too far. He was about to text an apology when Sarah replied, *I'll help you think about your job again. I've finished analyzing the telemetry data. There was an induced power surge on board your aircraft when the turbulence occurred. It sent all of the electronic systems haywire including the navigation system, the FADEC, the fly-by-wire and the autopilot. That turbulence wasn't turbulence. Someone sabotaged the plane.*

His smile vanished. *Someone on board?*

I don't know. I'm working with airport security and the regular TSA to figure out if anything happened on the ground. Keep alert.

He frowned and scanned the cabin again. Nothing looked suspicious at first glance. Bashir was out of his seat, consoling another passenger.

No, not consoling. He was leaning back in his seat talking to another passenger, but the other passenger didn't appear nervous. He had a serious expression and was leaning close to Bashir and whispering something into his ear. He wore a very well-tailored suit and shoes that looked to be custom made kid leather.

Alex frowned. The suit wasn't quite Wall Street, but it wasn't economy class either. What was someone so well-dressed doing in such a cheap seat?

He got up and headed toward the front of the plane. One of the flight attendants caught him and said, "Excuse me, sir, the captain has turned on the seatbelt sign."

Damn it. Alex should have remembered that. "Can I just use the restroom, please? I really need to go." *Say no. No special privileges.*

"No, I'm sorry, sir. You'll have to wait a little longer."

Alex sighed with relief but disguised it as irritability. "All right."

He took his seat again and made eye contact with the flight attendant. She took the hint and headed to the front to call the cockpit and ask for the seatbelt sign to be taken off.

Bashir finished his conversation with the well-dressed passenger. He looked back and made brief eye contact with Alex.

An alarm went off in Alex's head even as he smiled and lifted his hand in a perfunctory greeting. Bashir offered a slightly contemptuous smile of his own. A rich man disgusted by a commoner? Or a threat irritated at being suspected.

Either way, Bashir had caught him staring. That was bad. Alex would need to talk to him to dispel suspicion.

That was all right. He could also investigate a little further and see if there was anything to worry about from the attendant.

He began to wish the flight had been boring after all.

CHAPTER SIX

The seatbelt sign turned off a moment later, and the head flight attendant announced, "Okay folks, the captain has turned off the seatbelt sign. You are now free to move about the cabin."

"Oh, thank God," Alex said, getting to his feet and heading for the rear restroom. He sighed in frustration while secretly cheering his good fortune when a passenger beat him to it.

He turned around and started for the front restroom. The well-dressed passenger tensed slightly at his approach. Alex pretended to trip into him.

"Whoa!" He pressed his hand to the man's left breast and put the other on his right hip, checking for weapons while pretending to steady himself. No weapons. Not in the most likely places, anyway.

The passenger grunted and irritably pushed Alex away. "Do you mind?"

"Sorry," Alex said. "Don't have my sea legs, I guess."

"Well… Go away."

Alex offered him a smile and headed for the restroom, somewhat reassured. The man looked upset but not nervous. Just a rich asshole pissed that he had to share a cabin with poor folks.

He turned to Bashir and found the man staring daggers at him. That caused his suspicions to grow again. Once more, though, he couldn't be sure. Was he just upset at the possibility of trouble between passengers? Was he offended at someone with poor traveling etiquette?

Or was he concerned that Alex might not be who he seemed to be the way Alex was concerned that Bashir wasn't who he seemed to be?

He reached the restroom and found it empty. He walked inside, locked the door and texted Sarah.

Possibly a suspicious passenger. Check 15G.

He flushed the toilet and washed his hands to complete the ruse, then walked outside. He put a relieved smile on his face, as though he had just taken care of urgent business. When he passed Bashir again, he stopped and pointed.

Bashir stiffened and there was definitely anxiety in his expression. Alex kept the gesture for a moment longer to intensify that anxiety and throw Bashir off balance.

"Do I know you?" he asked.

"No, sir," Bashir said in a clipped voice.

"You sure? Did you go to Archibald High?"

"No, sir. I've never seen you before."

"Come on, I know I recognize you. I've been staring at you the entire flight."

Bashir relaxed slightly. This guy just lacked self-awareness and thought he knew Bashir. He wasn't suspicious of anything. "No, we've never met. I *have* noticed you staring at me, though. Glad to know it's a simple misunderstanding and not that you're incredibly rude."

Alex laughed. The corners of Bashir's lips turned down. Again, it could be simple disgust, but the anxiety he had shown earlier made Alex feel differently. "Come on. New York University?"

"N…" He frowned, then said reluctantly. "Yes."

"That's it! You played…" he looked Bashir up and down. Average height, trim build, most of his weight in his upper body. Chest and arms still defined though he was in his forties. "Water polo, right?"

Bashir sighed. "Yes. I played water polo."

"Ha! That's where I remember you. You played for the champions in 2001."

"No. I graduated in 2000."

"Really? No way you weren't on the team in 2001. You look just like the… the uh… the goal-scorer. What's the name of that position?"

"Either center or wing, usually."

"You were the wing, right? The left wing!"

"Yes. I was the left wing."

"I knew it! You sure you graduated in 2000?"

"Yes, pretty sure," Bashir replied drily.

"Maybe I have the years wrong. Did you win the championship in 2000?"

"No. We were defeated in the semifinals."

"Huh. I guess I'm thinking of a different guy. Hey, did you have Chemistry 101 with Professor Hildebrandt?"

Bashir lifted his hands and let them drop. His attitude was now one of complete irritation with no hint of anxiety at the peppering of questions from this annoying asshole who should just take his damned seat already. "I don't know. I don't remember Chem."

"Then no. Trust me, you'd remember Hildebrandt. Sixty years old but dressed like she was twenty and *far* better-looking than she was. Used to flirt with me all the time. Believe me, uncomfortable."

"I think I know what you mean. I often find unwanted attention uncomfortable."

Alex blithely ignored the hint and probed again. "That was some turbulence we had earlier, huh?"

Bashir's shoulders tensed. "Yes, it was.

Got him. He's involved.

Alex's senses went to high alert. He glanced casually back to the cabin. The well-dressed passenger was ignoring the conversation, but Alex thought there was something intentional in his ignorance.

He turned back to Bashir. "Weird that there was such powerful turbulence after the cabin said there'd be no weather. I mean, I know there are air pockets in clear skies sometimes, but still, you'd think that with today's technology, they could tell if we were going to fly into turbulence that strong."

"Weather's unpredictable sometimes."

"You know what I found really strange? The airplane banked twice. Not a lurch either. Two long, slow banks. I've never been in turbulence like that before. I've never heard of turbulence lifting the nose and pushing the aircraft into a climb either. That seem weird to you?"

Bashir stiffened a little more and refused to make eye contact. "Yes. Weird. But I'm sure it's nothing to worry about."

The chief flight attendant poked her head out. "Is everything…" She saw Alex and stammered a little. "Um… is everything all right?"

"Fine," Bashir said, eager to have an excuse to stop talking. "Sir, can you take your seat please? I don't mean to be rude, but I have some important business matters to attend to before lunch, and I'd appreciate it if you gave me some space."

"Right. Well," He clapped Bashir on the shoulder, moving his thumb to the front to check for the presence of a holster. Nothing there. "Nice talking to you Raj. Go Bobcats?"

Bashir managed a thin-lipped smile. Alex held his gaze a moment longer, then headed back to his seat. When he took it, his seatmate said, "Lunch? Why didn't you wake me up? I want lunch."

"The flight attendant said you can use the call button and order something. It's all premade anyway, you won't have to wait."

He pulled out his phone and angled it so the older man couldn't see it. Then he texted Sarah. *Bashir definitely suspicious. Likely involved with sabotage. Need info ASAP.*

Sarah texted back a moment later. *Working on it. Have info on 15G but nothing suspicious so far. Ishmael Mahmoud, 29, works as an account manager for Graystone Investment. They're a financial management firm.*

I'm familiar. Background?

Iranian national. Came to the U.S. seven years ago. Stayed on work visa, got his citizenship last year. No hint of ties to extremism.

Can you confirm his identity?

I can confirm that Immigration thought his ID was good. Can't really talk to Iran.

He frowned and looked back up at the passenger in 15G. He was doing something on his laptop, but from this distance, Alex couldn't tell if it was something suspicious. He doubted it. It wouldn't be smart to plan a hijacking on a laptop in full view of other passengers.

Was this a hijacking? It didn't have to be. The energy pulse could have been to disguise a financial crime. The airplane's Wi-fi recorded everything anyone did on the network, and there were aircraft systems that could detect when someone was connecting to satellite internet. They could be involved in white-collar theft and just needed the watchdog to blink while they sent a transaction.

That was reaching for an explanation, though, and Alex knew it. If they were involved in white-collar, they would have saved their business for the ground, not risked getting caught in the air.

He looked around the rest of the cabin. No one else seemed suspicious. The terror from the turbulence earlier had faded completely. People who weren't sleeping were waiting impatiently for their lunch or watching something inflight. A few were still reading books, determined to finish the paperback they had bought at the travel store before the flight ended.

Alex didn't like this. He couldn't just pull Bashir and Mahmoud aside and interrogate them. There was no way to do that unnoticed, and inducing panic on a flight could be catastrophic. Plus, there was always at least a slim chance that he was wrong, and if he was, then it would result in the end of his career and probably a lawsuit against the Air Marshals for profiling.

But something was up with them. He was sure of it.

Emma served his lunch, and he put a placid smile on his face and accepted the sandwich. She smiled at him and in spite of the tension he felt, warmth spread through his body. "Enjoy your meal."

"Thank you."

The protein box actually was pretty good. For airplane food, anyway. He ate quickly, scanning the cabin as he did. Still nothing suspicious.

Bashir glanced Alex's way and frowned sourly. Alex waved cheerfully to keep in character, and Bashir pointedly ignored him.

After the sandwich cart passed Bashir, he got up and walked over to Mahmoud again, Alex kept his eyes on them. Mahmoud frowned and said something to Bashir. Bashir frowned back. The two of them talked for a moment, then Bashir sighed and headed back to his chair irritably. Mahmoud lifted his hands and let them drop, then shook his head.

Alex relaxed slightly. They were probably business associates, and Bashir was irritable because Mahmoud was giving him bad news.

Maybe they were clean after all.

But no, Bashir had definitely acted suspicious. He definitely wasn't on the up and up. Maybe he wasn't planning to hijack the plane, but he knew something about that sabotage earlier.

A horrible thought occurred to Alex. Maybe the sabotage wasn't meant to take the plane but to bring it down. There were several high-profile accidents in the past decade related to technological malfunction. Maybe Bashir intended to crash the plane, and he was irritated now because it hadn't worked.

The silver lining in that case would be that they were probably safe now. The surge had passed, and Hollister had retained control of the aircraft.

The cloud within that silver lining would be that Bashir was still on the plane. If he couldn't get to the cabin, he could still get to an emergency door and cause explosive decompression. The plane would survive, but it was a good bet that a lot of passengers wouldn't.

Alex would have to risk making people nervous. He needed to restrain Bashir.

He reached for his seatbelt to do just that when he saw Mahmoud stand suddenly and reach into the overhead compartment. He frowned and waited a moment.

Mahmoud pulled out a leather briefcase and calmly disengaged the locks. Alex's eyes narrowed.

The briefcase opened, and Mahmoud pulled out a low-profile machine pistol.

Damn it!

Alex's hand flew to his shoulder holster, but a split second before he could draw his weapon, Bashir reached under his seat and came up with a similar looking weapon.

"All right!" he shouted. "The next person to move dies!"

He looked directly at Alex. Alex took his hand out of his jacket quickly, praying that Bashir didn't see him reaching.

Goddamnit. It was a hijacking. And they had gotten the drop on him.

<h1 style="text-align:center">CHAPTER SEVEN</h1>

A passenger screamed. Then another. A flight attendant joined them, and her eyes flew to Alex. Alex shook his head and prayed that she would know better than to reveal him. Her lip trembled, but she looked away.

"Good news, assholes and whores," Bashir said. "You all behave, and you all live. We're not *jihadists*, we're businessmen. This is for profit, not religion, and there's no profit in murdering people for no reason. That being said, there's no profit in letting one of you fuckers get in our way, so everyone take a fucking seat now!"

One of the flight attendants started toward him, and he swung the gun to him, snarling.

"God!" the flight attendant cried. "I'm just taking a seat in one of the crew chairs!"

"Not by passing me, you aren't. Sit on the damned floor!"

"Bashir," Mahmoud called to Bashir. Evidently, that was his real name. "Keep the aisles clear."

Bashir/Bashir frowned. "All right. Jeff, walk to the opposite aisle and keep your hands above your head. You can go to the front that way. You so much as sneeze at me, I'll swiss cheese your head, you got it?"

"Got it," the flight attendant said, voice trembling. "I just want to get home, man."

"That's wonderful. Who else wants to get home to their families?"

A choking sob came from somewhere on the plane. Alex followed the noise and found to his dismay that it came from the young mother. She clutched her son to her breast and stared at the two terrorists in abject terror.

"I asked a fucking question!" Bashir shouted.

The passengers all answered in the affirmative, and Bashir nodded. "Outstanding. So do I. So let's behave, and we can all go home to our loved ones. Sit down and enjoy your flight. By the way, we're heading somewhere else. You don't want to go to Dubai anyway, it's a den of iniquity, right, Mahmoud?"

Mahmoud—Mahmoud, it turned out—glared at Bashir. "Be quiet."

Bashir's crazed smile faded. Mahmoud took over and said, "I won't insult anyone's intelligence by acting like we're good men at heart. We're here to take something. It's none of your business what that is, and if it was, we wouldn't care. The reason you're alive is because, as my friend said, it's not profitable to kill you. The reason you'll stay alive is because you'll make sure it stays profitable not to kill you. Change that equation, and I will lose no sleep slaughtering any or all of you."

"Where are we going?" one of the braver passengers asked. "What are you going to do with us?"

"Where I say and what I say," Mahmoud replied without hesitation.

"Please," the mother cried. "I have a child."

"Are you married?" Mahmoud asked.

The woman blinked. "N—no."

"Then you're a harlot and your child is a bastard. If you can't keep your legs shut, do yourself and your bastard a favor and keep your mouth shut."

The woman sobbed and clutched her son tighter to her chest. Mahmoud looked at Alex and Alex must have shown some of his anger because Mahmoud aimed his machine pistol at him. "You. New York University."

Alex blinked and put a touch of false fear in his demeanor. "Me?"

"Yes, you. You didn't like that I called the unwed mother a harlot?"

Alex thought about his answer. He needed to be careful not to anger Mahmoud further, but his answer needed to be believable. He decided the most believable response was being too afraid to admit the truth.

It worked. As Alex expected, Mahmoud shouted, "Answer me!"

"No," Alex said, lifting his hands above his head. "No, I didn't."

"Hmm. Well, tough shit. This might not be a jihad, but that doesn't mean Allah smiles upon you. You're all infidels and sinners. Now you'll suffer the reward for your sin. Be careful not to earn a greater reward. Should I expect trouble from you, New York University?"

"No," Alex said. "No trouble."

"Good. Sit right there, and if you need to pee again, piss yourself."

A head poked out of the curtain to business class. Another passenger that Alex had only glimpsed briefly when he boarded. "We have the cockpit, Mahmoud. Keep economy class in line. No shooting unless you have no choice, but don't hesitate if you must."

"Yes, Yusef."

So Yusef was superior to Mahmoud was superior to Bashir. The terrorists had a hierarchy.

Alex took a moment to assess the situation. He needed to get a hold of Sarah, but he needed to do it when Mahmoud wasn't staring daggers at him. If he reached for his phone now, he would probably be shot. If he didn't respond to Sarah, she'd figure out something was up, but if they couldn't contact each other in some way, then he wouldn't know what she was learning or how to use that information.

That was step one. He needed to establish communication with Sarah. He had an earpiece in his jacket pocket. If he could get that in his ear, he could talk to her over satellite.

The problem with that was that there was no way to hide that from the terrorists. If the terrorists knew that the federal government was aware of them, then they might panic and start harming passengers.

He could try to get to the bathroom, but he had no doubt Mahmoud was serious when he admonished Alex to "piss himself" if he needed to pee.

He needed a distraction. He needed a reason for the terrorists to look away so he could text Sarah the situation.

The plane started to bank, and several of the passengers screamed as the reality of their situation reasserted himself. They were turning off course. They really were going to fly somewhere other than Dubai. They really were being kidnapped and held hostage.

"Shut up!" Bashir shouted. "I swear to God, I'll shoot your throats out to shut you up!"

Alex noted the tension in Bashir's body. Shoulders lifted high and pinched, knuckles white on the weapon's hand grip, legs shaking a little, lips pulled back over teeth. He was nervous.

In contrast, Mahmoud looked ice-cold. He was relaxed and stood with good posture, his fingers steady and relaxed on the trigger of his weapon. He was the one to worry about.

Not "the" one. There was Yusef, and then there was at least one other in the cockpit. More likely than not, there was a fifth terrorist in First class.

And possibly more. He could only see the two in front of him. It was possible there were two for each class and two in the cockpit. Hell, it was possible that members of the crew were involved.

No, probably not crew members. If crew members were involved, then Bashir and Mahmoud would have known he was the Air Marshal and either killed or neutralized him immediately.

That would be step two. Once he had a connection with Sarah, he would need to know the scope of the problem.

There was only one of him, and he was the only person armed. Pilots sometimes carried guns, but even in the post-9/11 world, it was rare, and he would have been informed if any of the crew was carrying.

He had a Glock 19 Gen5 pistol with three thirty-three round double-stack magazines. The standard magazine size was seventeen, and he had argued with Pat for weeks before she finally allowed him to order his own high-capacity mags. He wanted more firepower for exactly these kinds of situations.

Except that this situation meant he faced at least five terrorists, at least two of whom were armed with some sort of non-magnetic version of TEC-9M machine pistols that could fire twenty-two rounds faster than he could fire two rounds. It was a safe bet the other three had them too. A direct firefight was out of the question.

That would be step three. Once he had contact with Sarah and an understanding of the threat he faced, he would need to make a plan to address it. If he could somehow get a hold of one of those machine pistols, it would level the playing field considerably.

He would need to be patient. They were over the Atlantic Ocean right now. They still had eight hours to go before they reached Dubai. They still had two hours to go before they reached land, and that land was the Sahara in Africa. It was possible they were selling the plane to some warlord in a third-world African country, but that was unlikely. Most likely, they were taking it somewhere in the Muslim sphere.

Mahmoud's cover was that of an Iranian national. That didn't necessarily mean he was, but it was easier to fake an identity without also faking one's nationality. Iran was still on poor terms with the United States, even if they weren't necessarily on warlike terms. Maybe that was their destination.

For what purpose, though? The manifest didn't reveal anyone important on the flight they could ransom. They could maybe get a few million dollars for the first-class passengers, but even for a poor country like Iran, that wasn't enough to justify all this effort and risk. There were powerful factions in the United States government that would jump at any excuse to wipe the Ayatollah's government off the map. Kidnapping civilians was a nice little package wrapped up in a pretty pink bow for the warmongers in Congress.

The problem with that was that a peaceful resolution to this would be detrimental to those warmongers. Tragedy would boost their platform, so they would be more likely to push for no negotiation and harsh, threatening language that might prompt their kidnappers to kill the passengers.

Feeling cynical today, are we?

He sighed. It didn't matter. Whether this was some sort of ploy by the Iranian government or a private attempt to extort money, the chances of the passengers surviving a landing in Iran were slim and the chances of them escaping unharmed were nonexistent. His job was to make sure it didn't get to that point.

He looked back at the terrorists. They were conversing with each other in Farsi, and speaking in low tones, focused entirely on each other. They believed they had cowed everyone into compliance and didn't need to worry about anyone resisting them.

Now was his chance.

He pulled his phone out. As he predicted, there were several worried messages from Sarah. The final one said, *If I don't hear from you in five minutes, I'll assume a hijacking and scramble Air Force jets.*

That was four minutes ago. He quickly replied, *No, Air Force. Situation volatile. Plane hijacked, at least four terrorists, estimate three to six more. My identity remains hidden. Working on a plan. Need options that don't escalate the situation.*

And while you're at it, he thought, *I'd like a house in Martha's Vineyard and a summer home in Beverly Hills.*

He put his phone away and noticed his seatmate staring at him wide-eyed. *Dammit.*

"Keep quiet," he said softly. "Don't mention I have a phone and don't make it obvious that you know what I am. Best to just ignore me."

The older man had given Alex exactly zero indications that he was capable of that kind of deception, but he nodded and surprised Alex by immediately looking back at the terrorists with a frightened expression and completely ignoring Alex.

Alex's phone buzzed a moment later.

Pat alerted. Not sure what options will de-escalate. Might have to wait until you land. Destination?

He replied, *Unknown. Possibly Iran if Mahmoud's nationality is legitimate. Motive financial, but I don't have details yet.*

As expected, Sarah was also less than enthused about the possibility of a landing in Iran. *Will need to arrange response if Iran is destination. If the destination is coastal, the response will be military. If it is inland, we will have serious problems.*

Alex appreciated that Sarah didn't sugarcoat things. Trying to convince him that things would be okay no matter where they ended up would be a waste of time. He knew as well as she did that they were in bad trouble.

Now, he needed to find a way out of it.

CHAPTER EIGHT

Bashir and Mahmoud talked for a few more minutes before Bashir nodded and headed for business class. The man sitting next to Alex shifted in his chair and tensed slightly. Alex gripped his thigh and squeezed, then shook his head. *Don't try to be a hero.*

The man glared at Alex as if to say, *Then why aren't* you *doing anything?*

Alex wasn't surprised by the reaction. People watched movies and expected Air Marshals to be action stars who could dance through the aircraft and take terrorists out effortlessly. The irony was that Alex *could* take the terrorists out effortlessly, difference in firepower notwithstanding. He just couldn't do it without serious collateral damage, in other words, multiple civilian deaths.

It wouldn't help if this man or any other passengers decided to be cowboys. People watched other movies and expected the average Joe to somehow turn into a superhero because he nobly tried to save others on the plane. No one seemed to think they would end up being the guy who was tragically murdered after a pointless attempt at rescuing the plane.

So, he shook his head again, then lifted a hand just enough to make his meaning clear without broadcasting the gesture to Mahmoud. *Be patient.*

Unfortunately, Mahmoud picked up on the conversation anyway. "New York University! What are you talking to your grandfather about?"

The middle-aged man reddened at the insult, but thankfully stayed quiet. Alex lifted both hands into view and said, "Nothing. I was worried about my family back home."

He didn't think the terrorists would give a shit about the human impact of their actions, but if he could portray himself as a simple family man, it might make them worry less about him.

"You have a wife?"

"Yes. And two children."

"Do they behave?"

"Yes. All three of them."

Mahmoud smiled slightly. "An American wife who behaves? I don't believe you. I think you are trying to appeal to my religious nature."

"She's a stay-at-home Mom. She cooks, she cleans—"

"She fulfills your needs in bed? No complaining? Anything you ask, she gives her body to you as is the duty of a wife to a husband?"

Alex blinked and stammered, careful to make his shock seem genuine.

Mahmoud laughed. "I don't care, New York University. I couldn't care less about your sex life or your children. But it's clear you do. So do as we say, and when we have what we need, you can go home and enjoy your wife's obedience."

"Fucking asshole," Alex's neighbor whispered.

Alex kicked his calf to shut him up, but it was too late. Mahmoud cocked his head and strode swiftly toward him, machine pistol aimed directly at the man's head. "What's that? What did you say?"

Please don't say anything.

"You said I was a fucking asshole? Is that what I heard?"

Mahmoud stood right in front of Alex and jammed the gun right to the older man's head. "Speak up, old man, I couldn't hear you.

He was right next to Alex and leaning over, off balance. It would be effortless for Alex to disarm and subdue him. Then he could take the weapon and walk through the cabin to dispatch the terrorists.

But not without getting passengers killed in the process. His lips thinned, but he kept still.

Mahmoud chuckled and said, "Old man, tell me exactly what you said, or I'll kill random people until you do."

The man met Mahmoud's eyes, his own expression blazing with hate. "I said you're a fucking asshole."

"That's what I thought you said. Thank you for your honesty. And you're right. To you, I'm a fucking asshole. That's why I'll shoot your testicles off if you open your mouth again."

He pulled the weapon away and walked toward the front, arriving just as Bashir returned to coach. The two of them began talking in Farsi again, their backs turned to Alex.

Alex looked at his seatmate and frowned. The older man met Alex's eyes a moment, then lowered his gaze and nodded. He would be more careful now.

Alex pulled his phone out. A message from Sarah. *Need to confirm destination ASAP.*

That would be a risk, but one Alex would have to take. He would have to talk. He called out, "Where are you taking us?"

"Wherever I feel like," Mahmoud said without turning around.

"Look, I have money. I mean, I don't, but my brother does. He can give you—"

"If we want your money, we'll let you know."

"Just tell me where—"

Mahmoud spun around, aiming the pistol at Alex again. "Talk again, and *you'll* go straight to Hell!"

Alex clammed up. *So much for that.*

He waited for Mahmoud to turn around again, then texted Sarah. *They're not saying. They speak Farsi to each other, so I can't eavesdrop. I'm still thinking Iran.* After a moment, he sent a second text. *Check satellite feed and plot possible landings.*

If Sarah could track the plane through GPS, they could make some estimates of where the jet was most likely to land. Considering that the jet had a range of over fifteen hundred miles greater than their planned destination, that wouldn't help much until they got closer. At the moment, they could be flying anywhere from Cape Town to Moscow.

His phone buzzed, but it wasn't a response from Sarah. The message he had just sent was marked as undeliverable. In addition, the last message from Sarah was simply an indication that a message failed to download. He was cut off.

That was why Bashir had left coach. He had gone to the cockpit to tell them to cut off the plane's communications. It was likely that the plane flew completely dark now. They might not even have been targeting communications. All electronic flight systems generally went through a main bus with a single backup for essential systems like weather radar and navigation. The terrorists probably wanted to make sure the plane couldn't be tracked, and losing communications was just a byproduct of that.

Not that it helped him in any way. He couldn't contact Sarah, and Sarah just went from having a very poor idea of where the plane was going to absolutely no idea.

The terrorists had them completely at their mercy.

He wasn't sure that he believed them about this being profit related and not ideological. Certainly, their use of constant profanity suggested they weren't devout. However, zealots often weren't devout. Far too often, they were simply drunk on significance, caught up in the romance—and yes, that was the right word—of their cause. Like any other societal outlier, a zealot found comfort in exclusion.

You think I'm a lesser person but Allah (or God, or Christ, or, for that matter, Zues or Quetzalcoatl) chose me and not you. You think you're the superior one, but I'm the one who has forgone your devotion to depravity and filthy lucre.

He glanced at his phone again. The good news was that his second, rather than his first text came back as undeliverable. The fact that Sarah responded indicated to him that she received the first text. It was still a barely educated guess that they were heading to Iran, but if they were, then there was at least a chance that they could prepare.

But realistically, what did that knowledge offer him with no ability to communicate? He couldn't do anything to set them up for success. She would have to handle everything, and she would have to handle it with no understanding of the situation on board the craft as it evolved. He would have to handle the situation on board with no understanding of what resources he could or couldn't expect from the ground.

He was on his own. He was on his own, except for the hundreds of people counting on him to save them.

Seventy feet or so. The pilot didn't give a countdown. He just repeated, "Oh fuck oh fuck oh fuck oh fuck oh FUCK!"

They were all going to die. Every one of them. In a very odd way, Alex felt a measure of comfort in that. If he was going to die, he wanted to die with his brothers.

"Hold on!" the pilot screamed. "Hold on!"

Alex felt a slight tremor in his leg and checked his phone hopefully. Nothing. There was nothing new in his texts or, for that matter, anywhere else. He'd felt some vibration from the plane.

He couldn't keep looking at his screen, either. Drawing any attention to himself would invite attention, and he'd already drawn enough. At the moment, he had his handgun. That wasn't nearly enough, but he had it. Attention could easily change that. If they learned he was armed, then he would very quickly either be unarmed or dead. The circumstances were bad enough now. He didn't want to imagine them if he were completely unarmed.

He put his phone in his pocket. He needed to stop thinking like an Air Marshal and start thinking like a SEAL. That was the only way he could accomplish anything right now. It was time for him to start thinking of this situation as a mission with an objective. It was time for him to adapt to changing circumstances without compromising the objective.

Before he could start thinking, though, the little boy sitting a few rows ahead and to Alex's right said, "Mommy, I have to go to the bathroom."

The mother stiffened and cast frightened eyes on Mahmoud and Bashir. "Not yet, sweetie. I need you to hold it, okay?"

"But I can't. Mommy, please!"

"Not now, sweetie. Please be quiet."

"But Mommy!"

This time, Bashir spoke. "Keep your bastard quiet, or I'll quiet him for you!"

The boy burst into tears and said, "But I just want to go to the bathroom! I don't want to pee my pants like a baby!"

"I don't give a shit," Bashir said.

"But—"

Bashir rushed toward the two, a snarl on his face. He pointed the gun at the mother's head, and she shrieked. "Please don't hurt my baby!"

"I'm not going to hurt him," Bashir snarled. He made eye contact with the little boy and said, "I'm going to shoot his mother in the head if he doesn't shut up. Pee your pants. I don't care. But scream again, and you'll watch your mother die."

"All right."

The voice came from the older man sitting next to Alex. He was standing up. Alex grabbed his arm, but the man yanked his arm from his grasp and strode toward Bashir.

"That's enough. He's a little boy, and he wants to use the bathroom. We get it. You're tough. You're dangerous. You don't need to bully a child just because he wants to use the toilet."

Bashir snarled and spun his weapon toward the man. The older man caught it and forced it up to the ceiling.

And Mahmoud shot him through the base of the skull. He collapsed to the floor, instantly limp.

The passengers screamed, and the mother shrank back and twisted, trying to protect her son with her body. Bashir pointed his gun at the two of them, but Mahmoud laid a hand on his shoulder and said something in Farsi. Bashir calmed and lowered his gun.

"Take your son to the bathroom," Mahmoud said to the mother. "While you're in there, teach him to be quiet."

The mother nodded, weeping and shaking. She got up and headed for the bathroom, carrying her sun and shielding his eyes so he wouldn't have to see the dead man on the floor.

"Bashir, clean this up. You made the mess, you clean it."

Bashir glared at Mahmoud but didn't dare challenge him. As he dragged the body away, Mahmoud met Alex's eyes. "You have a problem, New York University?"

I'm going to kill you for that. "No," he replied. "No problem."

"Good."

He returned to his post at the front of the cabin, leaving the plane in stunned silence. Any hope the others had was gone now.

They were in the hands of murderers.

CHAPTER NINE

An hour passed. The terrorists spoke little to each other, and when they did, it was in Farsi. They kept a more watchful eye on the cabin now that the threat of interception was minimized with the aircraft's navigation system shut down.

The passengers remained silent, all of them too frightened to commit the transgression of whispering to each other and ending up in trouble like Alex and his deceased companion. One brave woman tentatively asked if she could use the restroom as well and was told that she was not a child and should know better.

The child in question was now fast asleep, probably the best thing that had happened so far. He sat on his mother's lap with his head on her shoulder and was the only person on the airplane who appeared peaceful.

The plane had changed direction once, turning back east. Alex guessed that the initial turn south was to throw off any pursuers, probably to make them think the plane was headed for sub-Saharan Africa. Now that the plane wasn't being tracked by satellite, they were heading once more toward the Middle East.

That detour would have used about five hundred miles of their range, give or take. That still gave them way too much room to play with. Assuming the destination was somewhere in Iran, that extra thousand miles meant they could end up anywhere within the country.

Alex still couldn't contact Sarah. With the situation evolved the way it had, that was now step three. Step one was the previous step two: determine the full extent of the threat. Step two was to deal with the threat, at least to the extent necessary to reestablish contact with Sarah.

He wasn't intimately familiar with 787s, but he knew that the backup bus for flight systems was in a panel near the cockpit luggage hold in the relief crew cabin. If he could get to that, somehow, he might be able to return communications to the plane. If the terrorists really were only concerned with navigation, they might not notice if communications were back up. The communications satellites weren't the same as the GPS satellites that provided navigation. As long as they weren't actively tracking signals but were relying on what the airplane told them, he could get things back up and running without attracting attention.

But he needed to get to the relief cabin first, and that meant making his way through the terrorists. That probably meant killing some or all of them and somehow doing that without alerting the cockpit, which wouldn't be easy. It would be better if he could find a way there without needing to kill anyone.

He considered the terrorists he had seen so far.

Bashir was a hothead. Mahmoud was, at the moment, the only thing keeping him under control. If Mahmoud was gone, Bashir would rapidly escalate.

On the other hand, Mahmoud was very calm. Either he had military experience, or he was sociopathic. Or perhaps so zealous that he believed with his whole heart that Allah would bless him for being righteous.

Either way, he was calm. He had killed that passenger because he needed everyone to understand the fate that awaited them if they resisted. If all the passengers attacked the terrorists as one, they would lose the plane. Mahmoud needed people to know that many of them would die if they tried that so he could continue to hold out the carrot that all of them could survive if they just listened and waited.

He had killed that man, but he had made it very clear that he considered Bashir responsible. That was both a genuine rebuke to Bashir and another message for the passengers. *You can trust me. Keep your mouth shut, do as I say and don't challenge us, and I'll keep a handle on things so no one gets hurt.*

Yusef was an unknown quantity. Other than being apparently superior to Mahmoud, Alex didn't know anything about him. The business and first-class passengers had apparently caused less trouble than the coach passengers because Alex hadn't heard anything from ahead of coach besides the occasional messages Bashir relayed to Mahmoud from the cockpit.

That was the greatest unknown. Alex knew there were two terrorists in coach. He knew there were at least two others ahead of coach. He knew what Yusef looked like, but he didn't know if there were any more terrorists ahead, or what the hijacker in the cockpit looked like.

And he had to walk through all of that to get even a chance at talking to Sarah or taking this plane back.

"Are you going to kill us?" One of the passengers asked, breath hitching with fear as he looked at Mahmoud.

Mahmoud sighed and said patiently. "If you behave yourselves, you will survive. If you don't, you will die. I don't know how to say this more clearly."

"Where are you taking us?" another passenger pleaded. "What do you want?"

"I'm taking you somewhere else. I want you to be silent."

Bashir glared but kept quiet. That was good. Mahmoud had sufficiently tamed him.

"He said he has money," a third passenger begged, looking at Alex. "Can't you just hear him out?"

Mahmoud raised his pistol, and the woman cried out softly and shrank back in her chair. Mahmoud stared at her with contempt, then directed that stare to the other passengers.

"I can see that you all are too foolish to keep calm simply on pain of death. In the interests of peace, I will tell you everything you need to know. First, I am taking you somewhere that is not Dubai. You don't need to know where. Second, I will do with you what the people who are paying me have ordered me to do. You don't need to know what they have ordered me to do except to know that it is their intention and mine that you endure this ordeal and return home alive when it is over.

"What you need to do now is sit in your chair, stay silent, and wait. I don't care if you're hungry. I don't care if you need to use the bathroom. I don't care if you're afraid. It would be better if you all survive to our destination, but not the end of the world if you don't. You should know this by now since I've already shot one of you through the brainstem.

"This is the last I will talk about this. The next person who speaks without being spoken to dies. If someone has a heart attack in their seats, and one of you feels a need to alert me of the situation, I suggest you watch them die instead."

He sighed heavily at the end of that speech as though he'd just finished lecturing a group of unruly teenagers. Bashir chuckled, then looked nervously at Mahmoud to make sure he hadn't gone too far. Mahmoud didn't react, and Bashir grinned again, taking particular delight in staring at the most frightened of the passengers.

Alex turned his attention to the flight attendants. The chef sat with five of the attendants in the crew seats just behind business class. There were two flight attendants in first class and one in business. That left Emma, and two others in coach.

Emma stood in the aisle next to the weeping mother and her sleeping child. She had a hand on the mother's shoulder and kept her eyes on Bashir. Alex felt a touch of admiration when Bashir glared at her, and she held his gaze steadily without showing fear. She had been so nervous at the meeting, but some people found their strength when others were in danger. Emma was clearly one of those people.

Bashir frowned and took a step toward her but then glanced at Mahmoud and thought better of it. Instead, he said, "What are you looking at, whore?"

Emma held his gaze for several more seconds, then slowly looked away, but not down. Her chin remained held high, which only infuriated Bashir more.

Alex decided to target Bashir first. Mahmoud's goal was to control the passengers while Bashir wanted to dominate and terrify them. This combined with his temper and poor self-control made him the biggest threat he faced.

He would find a way to Bashir and take him out, then he would take Mahmoud out. Preferably, he could handle both terrorists without firing his weapon. They most often stood close together, so it shouldn't be too hard to do that. Aside from his handgun, he also had a combat knife. As a SEAL, he was trained to a high level of proficiency in use of that knife, since SEAL missions often required covert action.

He just needed to get close.

Mahmoud had threatened that he would let someone die if they were undergoing a medical emergency, but did he mean that? He had warned several times that anyone who talked would die but had yet to follow through. He had killed the passenger next to Alex, but only when that passenger behaved aggressively and began struggling for control of Bashir's gun.

He could justify that killing to his superiors, but perhaps they wanted everyone left alive short of that necessity. If they let someone die of a heart attack, would those same superiors be happy with that choice?

Only one way to find out.

He began breathing heavily, slowly at first, then with increasing rapidity. He opened his mouth and gasped, shaking in his seat and clutching his right fist to his heart.

"Dammit," he whispered.

The passengers around him started noticing. One of them called out. "Hey! He's having a heart attack!"

Mahmoud paled, and Alex felt a leap of encouragement. He was right. Mahmoud was bluffing about letting sick people die.

"Did you hear me? He's having a heart attack! Are you really going to let someone die?"

"Sit down and be quiet!" Mahmoud shouted, his façade cracking for the first time. "New York University, what's going on? Are you all right?"

Alex shook his head and stood weakly.

"Sit down!" Mahmoud said.

"I'm a doctor," another passenger called, raising her hand for attention. "If you could allow a flight attendant to retrieve the defibrillator, I can help him."

"I can get it," Emma said immediately. She cast a terrified look at Alex, no doubt motivated at least partly by the fact that he was their Air Marshal and the only chance in hell of them surviving this. "Just keep breathing. You'll be okay."

No, damn it. I'm okay now. I just need to get to them.

He wished that the civilians on the plane could understand basic counterterrorism tactics too. He couldn't exactly tell Emma what was really going on.

Mahmoud swore in Farsi, then said, "All right. New York, stay there. You, grab the defib. Doctor, be prepared to save his life." He swore in Farsi again, then said, "Of course someone has a fucking heart attack right after I tell you all to just let them die.

"Be calm, Mahmoud," another voice said. "I am also a doctor. I don't think this gentleman is having a heart attack."

Alex turned to see a passenger in a t-shirt, denim jacket and jeans stand and walk to him. The man looked around Mahmoud's age but shorter and of much slighter build. He smiled at Alex, and Alex decided he would just have to go for it. He'd pretend to panic and rush toward Emma to get the defib, then, when he reached Mahmoud, he'd give it the old college try.

Just before he turned to start running, the man opened his denim jacket, revealing another TEC-9 pistol. His benign smile hardened, and his eyes bored into Alex.

You have to be kidding me.

CHAPTER TEN

"Relax, sir," the terrorist said. "There's no need to panic."

Alex thought quickly. "Okay. Yeah. I'm feeling better now. It…" he burped. "I think it's just heartburn."

"Of course it is," the new terrorist said wryly. "Have a seat. Rest is important in your condition. Miss Emma, please bring this gentleman an antacid tablet and a cup of water. Mineral is better if you still have some."

He gestured to Alex's seat. As Alex approached, he backed off, keeping himself out of lunging reach so Alex couldn't reach for him. Alex reluctantly took his seat.

"I suppose there's no longer a need to disguise myself," the new terrorist said. "Our employers anticipated medical emergencies, so they hired me to accompany Yusef's crew. I am Doctor Hasam. If anyone has a medical emergency, please alert me. As Mahmoud said, it is better if you all reach your destination alive."

"It would have been nice for Yusef to tell me this," Mahmoud said irritably.

"Yes. I suggested he make everyone aware of our identities, but he is paranoid, you know. Don't let it concern you. You've done well."

Emma returned with the water and the antacid. She handed it to Alex, who reluctantly drank it and offered her a smile. She held his gaze a little longer than she should have, but the terrorists didn't notice. Fortunately, they weren't as perceptive as he was.

This wasn't a complete loss, at least. He now had a clearer understanding of the hierarchy. Yusef was the leader, and Hasam was something like a warrant officer. Not a part of the chain of command, per se, but wielding absolute authority in his field, in this case, medical. Mahmoud was probably the person in charge of coach, which was why he had been calling the shots until a medical issue arose.

The cloud to this silver lining was that if Yusef had kept that kind of vital information hidden from Mahmoud, then he may have kept other things hidden too. It was possible that Mahmoud didn't even know where they were going or why. That made Alex's job more difficult. He couldn't press just anyone for information. He needed to go straight to the top.

One rung at a time. He still needed control of coachcoach. He turned back to Hasam and found him smiling back, his eyes still hard. He looked less physically imposing than Bashir and Mahmoud, but far calmer. He had also demonstrated greater intelligence than either of the others by giving Alex no room to reach for his weapon.

Bashir was still the weak link. Getting to him would be very difficult, however, because now he had attracted attention to himself, and now Hasam would almost certainly watch him like a hawk. Possibly he already had. He might have been watching Alex from the beginning and only acted now when he caught Alex attempting a coup.

And Alex hadn't seen him. He hadn't seen Mahmoud or even Bashir. Not until it was too late.

No, that wasn't true. The moment he felt turbulence on the plane, he saw right through the Bashir's smug smile and knew he was up to no good. The issue wasn't that Alex hadn't seen the terrorists, the issue was that he had seen them and hadn't responded to them. He'd been cautious when he should have been active. He should have pulled Bashir aside right away and figured out what was going on.

Would that have helped though or would it have just meant things were accelerated. He couldn't have known enough to pull Bashir aside at gunpoint and prepare for other terrorists to show up with machine pistols. If he had done that, he probably would just have been shot by the others.

God, this was so frustrating!

"Are you all right?" Emma asked him.

He smiled at her. "Yes, I'm fine. The tablet helped a lot. Thank you."

"You're sure it was heartburn?" She looked up at Hasan and glared.

"I'm sure," Alex said. "I feel much better."

Emma looked at Hasan and said, "How can you do this? You swore an oath to do no harm."

Mahmoud frowned and said, "What did we say to you about speaking? That applies to you too, stewardess!"

Hasam smiled and shrugged apologetically and didn't respond to Emma's question. Emma glared at her, then looked back at Alex. "You're sure you're okay?"

"He's sure," Mahmoud said. "Leave him alone."

She glared at Mahmoud and reluctantly walked back to her place next to the crying mother.

Back to square one.

The passengers looked nervously at each other. Another layer had been added to their alarm. The terrorists were behaving confusingly. They wanted everyone silent and in their seats, but Alex had left his seat and he was still alive. They told them that no one could use the restroom, but that mother had been allowed to take her child. They said they wanted to kidnap the passengers, but they didn't hesitate to kill the one of them who resisted rather than simply subdue him, which they could have done just as easily. They didn't hesitate to kill a passenger, but despite Mahmoud's dire warning, they had acted to save someone undergoing a medical crisis and even had a doctor onboard to address just such an emergency.

Why did they have a doctor on board? That part confused Alex too. It really wasn't materially different to the terrorists if they brought all two hundred ninety-three civilians to their destination or just two hundred eighty of them. And if it was, why was it different? These were normal people. Even the wealthy ones weren't important people. What value came from keeping all of them alive?

The only thing Alex could think was that maybe this was some government-sponsored ploy to capture American citizens after all. Kidnapping Americans was tricky. The United States would be very reluctant to act harshly with its own citizens alive and in captivity. They would do everything possible to keep from acting in a way that would cause the terrorists to kill them. If the terrorists started killing people, then the United States was far more likely to act *very* harshly.

So the terrorists needed to be circumspect. They couldn't allow a revolt, but they needed as many people to survive unharmed as possible.

That meant they probably wouldn't be too harsh about allowing someone to use the restroom. And people with heartburn often had other stomach concerns.

He grimaced and put a hand to his midsection. Then he groaned.

Mahmoud rolled his eyes and said, "What now, New York University?"

Alex shook his head. "I'm fine." He grimaced again and grabbed his midsection. "No, I'm not. Dammit. I need the restroom."

"No," Mahmoud snapped. "No restroom."

Alex looked up at him with an anguished expression. "Man, I really need to go. If I don't get to the restroom quick, I'm going to leave a mess."

The passengers near Alex recoiled in horror and disgust. *They didn't cover* this *in training*, he thought drily.

More relevant were the thoughts of the terrorists. Judging by Mahmoud and Bashir's body language, horror was at the forefront of those thoughts as well, along with profound irritation and anxiety. Their image of a flawless takeover and effortless completion of their mission had been completely shattered. Mahmoud's almost unflappable calm had devolved into uncertainty nearly as great as Bashir's, though without the propensity to violence.

Speaking of propensity to violence, Bashir spoke to Mahmoud in Farsi. Alex couldn't understand the words, but it was clear by Bashir's gestures that he wanted permission to kill Alex. It was just as clear by Mahmoud's tone that he was denying Bashir that boon.

Alex turned to Hasam, who was regarding him calmly but now curiously. That wasn't good. He didn't want Hasam to wonder if he was something more than just an ordinary passenger.

He was committed now, though. "Doc, please. I'm sure you know that irritable bowel syndrome causes symptoms besides heartburn. I'll stay here if you want me to, but you guys are going to be dealing with some really unpleasant smells here in a moment, and unless everyone here has an iron stomach, you're looking at a lot of people contributing some other very unpleasant smells."

Hasam frowned. He *was* aware of those other symptoms. He looked at Mahmoud and spoke in Farsi.

"No, Damn it!" Mahmoud said in English before another stream of Farsi. Hasam replied calmly, and Mahmoud sighed. "Fine. You take him then. You want to be the restroom escort? Be my guest."

Predictably, several other passengers raised their hands.

"Wait your turn!" Mahmoud snapped. "Hasam, take New York University to the bathroom before he shits all over the plane."

Alex stood up and started forward, Hasam's gun in his back. When Alex reached Mahmoud, he would stab Mahmoud in the neck, then spin and stab Hasam. Bashir would be last, and there was a high risk he would get at least one burst off before Alex got to him, but it was the best he could do.

He would have to get each of them precisely where the brainstem met the spinal cord. It was the same place Mahmoud had shot the other passenger and would instantly put them down so there was no chance of their fingers stiffening on the trigger and hitting a passenger or putting a hole in the aircraft. Contrary to popular belief, shooting a small hole in the cabin wouldn't cause the entire airplane to explosively decompress, but it would be better if the passengers didn't panic.

That was the other risk. If the passengers panicked or cheered or made any kind of noise at all—which they certainly would—it could alert the other terrorists and make Alex's job of getting to the cockpit infinitely harder. He would have to very quickly hush the passengers to minimize that risk. It would be a close thing, no matter what.

Then, it wasn't a thing at all because Alex's plan wasn't a thing. Alex's plan wasn't a thing because instead of keeping his weapon trained on Alex, Mahmoud walked around the front of the cabin to the other aisle, putting too much distance between himself and Bashir for Alex to reach him with his knife. He would have to shoot Mahmoud after all.

Then he wasn't going to shoot Mahmoud because Mahmoud spoke in Farsi. Then he and Bashir pointed their weapons at other passengers. Alex felt the gun leave his back and knew that Hasam had done the same.

Mahmoud met Alex's eyes, a great deal of his calm returned now that he was in control of the situation. "I don't know who you are, New York University, or who you think you are, but if you try anything at all, we will kill these passengers. If you are a movie star badass, you might get one of us, but you won't get all three of us before innocent people die. So go take your shit if you really have to, then go back to your seat."

Damn it. Damn it all to hell.

"Okay," Alex said. "Fine. I'm not going to try anything."

He hurried ahead, but not to reach Bashir in time to act. He just needed to keep up the pretense that he was desperate for the lavatory.

He reached the restroom and locked it, then sat heavily on the toilet and put his head in his hands. "Christ, what a shitshow."

He had often wondered how terrorists had successfully hijacked flights in the past. When there were no Air Marshals aboard, he understood, but he didn't understand how Air Marshals could be so utterly incompetent at their jobs that terrorists could perpetrate such horrors as the 9/11 attacks.

He understood now. One person armed with a handgun and a knife—and most of them didn't even carry knives—couldn't hope to do anything against multiple terrorists armed with machine pistols.

Except he *could*, dammit! He could take all of them. He wasn't just an Air Marshal, he was an ex-Navy Seal. He was one of the most dangerous people on the planet, and it didn't matter if there were three or maybe six of them and one of him. He could handle all of them.

But not with civilians on board. Not with innocent lives caught in the crossfire. The terrorists intended to keep everyone alive if possible, and that meant that if he didn't have a surefire way to stop them without getting anyone hurt, the right thing for him to do was to stay acquiescent.

So once more, he and the nearly three hundred lives he was responsible for were at the mercy and whim of violent murderers.

"Damn it all to—"

The floor suddenly dropped out from under him. He cried out when his head hit the ceiling, then cried out again when he hit the floor. The aircraft groaned around him, and he could hear shouts and screams as passengers panicked.

The plane was falling from the sky.

CHAPTER ELEVEN

Alex got to his feet and quietly opened the lavatory door. Outside, pandemonium was ensuing. Hasam, Bashir and Mahmoud were screaming and shouting at passengers who panicked and left their seats. Several passengers lay unconscious in the aisles from hitting the ceiling when the plane dropped. Others wept, including the boy, who had woken probably from hearing his mother scream.

"Get down! Get back to your seats!"

"You're going to kill us!" a man accused them. "You're going to kill us all!"

"No, we aren't!"

"You're crashing the plane!"

"Sit the fuck down, or I'll kill you now!"

This was Alex's chance. Behind the curtain to business class, he could hear similar chaos. He slipped out of the restroom and started into business class. There were only two terrorists for economy to control nearly four times as many passengers as business class. If he got lucky, there would only be one terrorist in business class, and he could disable him and take his weapon.

He got lucky. There was only one terrorist standing at the front of business class. He shouted and waved his weapon at the business class passengers, who were indeed panicking. Alex joined them, flailing his arms and crying out, stumbling around as the plane continued to descend. The plane—still falling fast—banked sharply left just as Alex reached the front of business class.

The passengers all cried out and fell. The terrorist fell into Alex. His eyes met Alex's in surprise an instant before Alex snapped his neck.

Alex quickly lowered the body to the ground and retrieved the machine pistol, hiding it under his jacket. He looked around. No one had seen him.

He took the pistol and started toward first class, but the plane righted itself suddenly, pulling up and leveling out. The passengers kept crying but stopped screaming, and Alex could hear Mahmoud saying,

"Everyone back to your seats! We'll figure out what happened in a moment!"

That meant he was going to send someone to the cockpit. That meant someone was going to see Alex and wonder why he was in business class and not back in coach. Then they were eventually going to see the body of their friend and wonder why he was dead and who had killed him. It wouldn't be hard to put two and two together, and while he was much better prepared now that he had the machine pistol, he still couldn't risk a firefight.

He headed quickly back to coach. The three terrorists in coach had their backs turned to him, so he stepped into the lavatory again.

He tried to quell his disappointment. This was a good thing. He was far better armed now, and he had reduced the terrorist's numbers by one. That would drop their morale considerably.

There were risks associated with that. Their fear could lead them to kill passengers. But considering how important keeping them alive seemed to be, it was more likely that it would lead to disagreements amongst themselves that Alex could exploit.

This wasn't the coup d'etat he hoped it would be, but it was a major victory.

"Where is New York University? How long does it take him to shit?"

That was Bashir. Hasam replied with, "Maybe he broke his neck too."

Alex felt a pang when he heard that. Evidently, some of the passengers weren't just unconscious.

"Go check on him, Bashir," Mahmoud said. "If I hear a gunshot, the second one will be to your own head. Understand?"

Bashir muttered something angry in Farsi, then slammed his gun on the lavatory door. "Hey! Are you dead?"

"No," Alex said groggily. "Just hit my head."

"Are you finished in there?"

"Yeah. Yeah, hold on. I'll come out."

He opened the door and stumbled, taking care to come close to Bashir without actually touching him and giving him a chance to discover the new weapon he had tucked into his belt underneath his jacket.

Bashir jumped back and kicked Alex's thigh.

"Hey!" Alex cried. "What did you do that for?"

Bashir lifted his gun to Alex and snarled. "Back to your seat!"

Alex lifted his hands and headed back to his seat. "Okay! Okay! Hey, what the hell happened just now?"

He looked at the other two terrorists and saw that they were once more aiming their guns at other passengers. *Damn it!* These guys were the oddest mix of incompetent and professional.

With the option of killing these three without endangering innocents unavailable, he made his way back to his seat. He shared a look with Emma as he passed her. Her eyes asked a question she couldn't answer.

He sat, and Mahmoud said, "Bashir, go to the cockpit and figure out what happened. If those pilots are fucking with us, kill everyone but the captain."

The crew, apparently, weren't as valuable as the passengers.

Alex rubbed his head, which really was sore after hitting the ceiling, and Emma walked to him. She knelt in front of him and asked, "Are you hurt? Do you need to go somewhere and lie down?"

What she was really asking was if she could take him somewhere the terrorists couldn't see him. He appreciated the thought, but he wasn't ready to be out of sight yet. If he was missing when they found the other man's body, it would look suspicious.

He shook his head and said, "No, I'm fine." Then he opened his jacket, revealing the TEC-9. He rubbed his chest and said, "Heartburn's still acting up, but not too bad."

Emma's eyes widened for a moment, but she didn't react otherwise. She looked at Alex with a spark of hope, understanding exactly how Alex had obtained that weapon. "Well, if you need anything, let me know."

He took his hand from his jacket and closed it again. "Thank you. I'll ride this out for a while and let you know if I need another antacid."

She smiled at him, and despite the circumstances, he noticed how beautiful she was once more. She returned to her place at the mother's side and put a hand on the little boy's shoulder. The sniffling boy looked up at her gratefully, still clinging to his mother.

Alex looked around the cabin. Three passengers lay in the aisles. One of them had clearly broken his neck. The other two didn't have any visible injuries, but it was clear they were both dead as well.

That was at least four passengers dead so far, and one terrorist. This was already a tragedy. The best Alex could hope for now was preventing this tragedy from turning into a catastrophe.

What had happened to the plane? Had the terrorists' tampering with the plane's systems caused things to go haywire? Had they actually hit a really big air pocket this time? Or had the pilots actually tried to sabotage the flight somehow?

Bashir returned to the cabin and spoke to Mahmoud. Hasam started back toward the rear of the cabin but stopped when Mahmoud held his hand up. It seemed Mahmoud was superior to Hasam in every respect but medical questions.

Once more, they spoke in Farsi, so Alex couldn't hear what was being said. The frown on Mahmoud's face suggested that whatever the explanation was, it wasn't satisfactory.

"What the hell happened?" another passenger asked.

"Quiet, infidel," Mahmoud replied without looking.

"Look, if I'm going to die, I'd rather get shot than die in a plane crash, so either shoot me or tell me what happened."

Still without looking, Mahmoud asked, "Hasam, do you have a first aid kit with you?"

"I do."

"Good."

Mahmoud turned to the passenger and shot him in the knee. The passenger—a younger man, perhaps twenty-four or -five, cried out and dropped to the ground. He stared in horror at his ravaged knee, then screamed.

Mahmoud stood over him and smiled pleasantly. "It seems there was a minor technical issue with the flight control surfaces that caused the airplane to lose control briefly. We have the situation under control now. There's nothing to worry about."

Still smiling, he shot the passenger's other knee. Alex had to fight to keep from grabbing his confiscated machine pistol and emptying the clip into Mahmoud.

The passenger screamed and writhed on the floor, eyes huge in disbelief. Hasam made eye contact with Alex as he passed him and held it until he retrieved his first aid kit and headed back to the front of the cabin.

Mahmoud turned to Bashir and issued another command. Bashir tore his crazed smile from the crippled man and headed for business class.

Alex braced himself. They would discover the dead terrorist soon. He would have to figure something out quickly or they would determine the truth. Maybe because his neck was snapped, they would assume he died during the turbulence.

But his weapon was missing.

Alex swore inwardly. He should have left the gun. He couldn't use it right now, and its absence not only on the body but the rest of the business class passengers would spark suspicion. Clearly, the terrorists being on edge wasn't the good thing Alex thought it would be. He could have gotten people killed with his choice.

Hindsight was twenty-twenty. All he could do now was keep the weapon and wait for a chance to use it.

Bashir came back a moment later, a fearful look on his face. He whispered to Mahmoud, and Mahmoud's eyes popped to him. "What?"

Bashir flinched backwards and repeated what he had said, a little more hesitantly this time.

Mahmoud swore. "Damn it!" He looked around at the passengers, and his eyes fixed on Alex. Alex maintained an innocent stare and hoped that Mahmoud would buy it.

Mahmoud sighed and looked back at Bashir, then at Hasam. Hasam continued to bandage the weeping passenger's knees, but his deep frown betrayed his concern.

"Damn it." Mahmoud said something in Farsi, and Bashir headed to business class.

Alex heard shouting coming from business class as Bashir interrogated the passengers. Mahmoud said something to Hasam, and the doctor stood. Mahmoud issued another command, and Hasam nodded and went to business class.

Bashir returned and spoke to Mahmoud briefly before they both addressed the crowd. "Who the hell killed him?"

The passengers looked at each other in confusion, and Mahmoud said, "Enough playing stupid. Someone killed my friend Abdul. Who the hell did it?"

No one answered. Mahmoud glared at everyone and said, "All right. That's fine. No one wants to talk? We'll make you talk. Hasam. Go to business class. You're in charge there now. Bashir. Go get a hostage."

Alex's heart sank to the floor when Bashir turned his eyes to Emma and grinned lecherously.

Oh God. What have I done?

<h1 style="text-align:center">CHAPTER TWELVE</h1>

Alex' stiffened as Bashir grabbed Emma by her hair and yanked her to her feet. The woman she had been comforting said, "No! Leave her alone!"

Bashir pointed his gun at her and said, "Be quiet, whore!"

The little boy started crying again, and Bashir reddened. Before he could do anything rash, though, Mahmoud called, "Bashir! Bring her here!"

Bashir spun around and dragged Emma after him. When he reached the front, he turned around and dragged Emma to the ground, then pointed his pistol at her. Emma grimaced from the pain of having her hair pulled but kept a brave face.

Alex couldn't quite say the same for himself. He cried out, "Hey! What the hell are you doing?" completely forgetting the need to avoid attracting attention to himself.

Mahmoud focused rage-filled eyes on him but addressed the entire cabin. "Someone killed our comrade in business class. Someone's going to admit to that crime, or we're going to kill all of the pretty women on this plane, starting with this one."

"Hold on," Alex said. "Three passengers in coach died from the turbulence. How do you know that's not how your friend died? You all hit the ceiling too, right?"

Mahmoud frowned, and Alex pressed his advantage. "How did he die anyway? Was he shot? Stabbed?"

"His neck was broken."

"Then come on. You saw what happened to them." He pointed at the dead passengers still in the aisles, ignoring the guilt he felt at using them to defend Emma. "If they died from having their necks broken, then why couldn't your friend have died the same way? This was an accident."

"Maybe something's wrong with the plane," another passenger suggested. "Maybe when you guys took the cockpit, you shot something or broke something that messed up the plane so it's flying all crazy."

Mahmoud's expression faltered again. He shared an anxious glance with Bashir. As for Bashir, his face had gone ashen, and the hand holding the pistol to Emma's head trembled.

Mahmoud looked back at the passenger and said in an unsure voice, "We disabled navigation so no one could track us. But that shouldn't affect the airplane. It's piloted by people, not by computers."

So they weren't going after satellite communications after all. Just navigation.

Alex filed that information for future use and said, "Damn it, Mahmoud, these modern planes all fly by computers. The pilots turn the wheel and stuff, but all that does is tell the computers what to do. It's like a new car. You know how when you slam your pedal to the floor, there's a second before the car accelerates, and then it gradually ramps up power? It's the same thing. The computer decides how much power to give each engine and how much to turn each of the ailerons and flaps or whatever." Alex knew exactly what the control surfaces were, but New York University didn't, and he needed to maintain that façade. "If you mess with the computer, then you're messing with the plane's ability to fly."

Mahmoud's face paled another shade. "We didn't know that."

Time to go for the killing blow. "You need to fix this. I don't know how, but you need to bring the computers back online. If you don't, then these things are going to keep happening, and one of these times, the pilots aren't going to be able to rescue us. You'll lose this plane, you'll lose all of these passengers, and you'll lose your money."

Mahmoud looked at Bashir, and Bashir shrugged. Mahmoud looked at Emma, then said, "All right. Let her go. Then go to the cockpit, and—"

Yusef showed his face to coach for the first time since the terrorists had taken over the plane. He spoke to Mahmoud but spoke in English and loudly enough for everyone to hear.

"I spoke with Cyrus. The captain and first officer tried to crash the plane into the ocean. They thought we were going to make them crash into the Burj Khalifa. We've killed them and placed the relief crew in charge. For the sake of ease, I've told them that we're flying to Iran and will land safely at Bandar Abbas International Airport. There is no need for anyone to fear loss of their lives."

Relief washed over Mahmoud's face. It lasted only a moment, however. His eyes narrowed, and he looked at Alex.

"That doesn't mean your friend wasn't killed by the pilots when they tried to crash us. It was an accident. Emma didn't do anything."

"You know her name?" Yusef asked.

Alex studied him. Aside from a calm more unflappable than Mahmoud's or Hasam's had ever been, he carried himself with the erect bearing and natural command of a leader. His eyes were shrewd as well. They bored right through Alex, and Alex could tell he was looking right through every deception Alex was trying.

"It's on her nametag," Alex said.

"It is, but that's not how you know her name."

It wasn't a question.

"I'm just saying there's no need to shoot her. Christ, haven't enough people died? You guys won. You have the airplane. You don't need to kill us. What are we going to do?"

"Most of you will do nothing," Yusef said. "You already have. I think you killed Abdul and stole his weapon."

Mahmoud and Bashir flinched. Rage crossed Bashir's face, and guilt crossed Mahmoud's. They both realized now that they should have killed Alex.

Well, they'd probably get their chance now.

"What the hell are you talking about?" Alex said. "I was in the bathroom!"

Yusef nodded. "Kill the woman."

Bashir snapped his weapon back to Emma, and Alex shouted, "Wait!"

Yusef held up his hand, and Bashir glared but refrained from pulling the trigger. "Yes?"

"You're right," Alex said. *Goddamnit.* "I killed Abdul and took his weapon."

He opened his jacket and pulled out the TEC-9, holding it by the back and keeping the barrel pointed at the floor and his hand away from the trigger. The passengers gasped, and a few cried, realizing how close to salvation they had come only to have it taken from them.

"I had to try," Alex said, hating the defeat he heard in his voice. "I had to try to stop you. You're capturing hundreds of innocent people, and if you're taking us to Iran, then you're risking war with the United States, which will result in tens of thousands of deaths, if not more. Many of them innocent civilians."

"So you admit that your country kills civilians!" Bashir spat.

"Civilians die in every war," Alex said. "Blame us if you want, but I didn't kidnap a plane full of Iranians and get four of them killed."

"You are the Air Marshal."

That was Yusef again. Once more, it wasn't a question.

Alex looked at Emma. She stared at him, defiance on her face, and shook her head. She was willing to die to protect his secret.

But he wasn't willing to kill her.

"Yes," he said softly. "I am."

The passengers gasped again, looking at him in shock. Many of those faces stared in accusation, all asking the same silent question. *How could you let this happen?*

Mahmoud looked at Alex with something akin to admiration. "You clever infidel," he whispered. "You had us completely fooled."

"He did," Yusef said, "and you and I will discuss the consequences of that later."

He alone showed no strong emotion. Alex could understand why Mahmoud tried to imitate him earlier. That level of calm was invaluable in a situation like this.

Mahmoud flushed guiltily but not fearfully. Apparently, the discussion wouldn't take place at the end of a gun barrel. He was pretty sure Mahmoud could kiss his promotion goodbye, though.

"You did well, Air Marshal," Yusef continued. We didn't know you'd be on the flight. That was good, although the credit for that likely lies with your superiors. You managed to keep your presence a secret, which was excellent. Despite being hopelessly outnumbered and outgunned, you somehow contrived a circumstance that placed you in the right place at the right time to attack one of us. That was outstanding. Best yet, you capitalized on that opportunity without overextending yourself and getting many of your fellow passengers killed. That was incomparable.

"Unfortunately, you blew your cover. You made a mistake taking Abdul's weapon. There is nothing you can do with it against all of us, not without getting many of your charges killed. Had you contented yourself with the death, we would have remained oblivious of you, and you could have sought other opportunities."

Alex stifled the rage that rose in his heart, but he couldn't stifle the guilt. Yusef was right. He had ruined everything by taking the machine pistol.

"Come forward, Air Marshal. What is your real name?"

No reason to lie anymore. "Alex."

"Alex. Come forward. Mahmoud, take Abdul's weapon and search him for his own weapons. Bashir, if he does anything he shouldn't, kill the woman."

"With pleasure," Bashir snarled.

Each step Alex took was like a step to the gallows. He glared at Mahmoud and received an equally hateful glare in return. It took all of his training not to snap Mahmoud's neck when the terrorist took the machine pistol.

Mahmoud patted him down roughly, and Alex kept his eyes on Yusef, taking the measure of the man. The calm he wore was given to him by experience. It didn't come from superiority, like Mahmoud's, or confidence like Hasam's. Yusef was calm because, despite the unforeseen events, he knew he was in control.

He was military. Maybe ex-, maybe active duty. He was in charge of this operation, and he was clearly the right choice for that assignment. Alex guessed his age at around forty, roughly the same as his own. He was in good shape, but not overly muscular like Mahmoud or sculpted like Bashir. He had the wiry, well-proportioned frame of a special operator.

Hollywood liked to portray special forces as thickly muscled super athletes with the physiques of bodybuilders and the height and mass of football players. The reality was that most special operators were of roughly average height and weight, stronger by far than an untrained person for sure, but not powerlifters. At six-foot-three and two hundred fifteen pounds, Alex was an outlier. Most Navy SEALs were five to eight inches shorter and thirty to fifty pounds smaller.

Alex would bet anything that Yusef was Iranian Special Forces.

Mahmoud removed Alex's pistol and knife and stepped away. "He's clean," he said to Yusef.

"Thank you. Alex, if you would follow me, please? I trust you will be intelligent enough not to try anything and guarantee the flight attendant's death."

Alex followed Yusef, casting one last look at Emma as the terrorist led him away. Emma refused to meet his eyes, her own narrowed in anger that he completely understood.

Yusef led him through business class. Hasam's eyes first widened, then narrowed when he saw Alex. When Yusef entered first class, a bald man around Alex's size and build looked at him, then at Yusef. He asked something in Farsi, and Yusef replied in English.

"Yes, this is the Air Marshal."

The first-class passengers reacted with the same shock as the coach passengers. Cyrus nodded. "He's responsible for Abdul?"

"Yes."

Cyrus looked Alex up and down. Like Yusef, there was no emotion in his gaze. He was probably a soldier too, or an ex-soldier. He said something else in Farsi, and this time Yusef's response was also in Farsi.

Cyrus switched to English for his next question. "Should I return to the cockpit once I bind him?"

"Yes. Keep him in the relief cabin. Tie his bonds to the luggage hold."

A rush of hope returned to Alex, and he fought to keep it from his face. They were going to tie him up right next to the secondary control panel. He could get a hold of Sarah again. He could tell her the situation and give her an exact destination.

These terrorists were about to learn exactly why you shouldn't mess with the United States.

CHAPTER THIRTEEN

Cyrus bound him quickly and professionally. Alex remained silent and complied with the terrorist's instructions. Aside from the futility of taking on all five remaining terrorists while weaponless, he had a real chance at a happy ending now. If he could get a hold of Sarah and let her know what to expect, they could land at the airport right in front of a U.S. response that would cow even the most fanatic members of the Iranian government.

When Cyrus finished tying him, he nodded to Yusef and walked into the cockpit. Alex caught a brief glimpse of Captain Hollister's and First Officer Grant's bodies. It pained him to know that they had died so heroically to prevent something that was never going to happen in the first place.

Alex risked questioning Yusef now. Yusef was confident. Maybe he would be confident enough to share their plans. "What are you going to do with us?"

"We are going to land at Bandar Abbas. At that point, you will be turned over to my employers. I truly don't know what the plan is after that, but it has been made clear to me that as many passengers as possible are to survive this journey. For the moment, that includes you and the flight crew as well. Understand, though, that if we must kill to reach Bandar Abbas we will."

"Yes, your boy told me that. I don't believe that you don't know what happens after that, though."

Yusef shrugged. "That is your problem, Alex. Not mine."

"Why take us alive? You're not going to get any ransom money."

"I will. I and my men will be paid very handsomely. I will see to it that Abdul's family receives his share. As for my employers, as I said, I don't know their goals. I didn't think it important for me to know, so I didn't ask."

"You mean your superiors, right? Your generals."

A ghost of a smile crossed Yusef's lips. "I am no longer Revolutionary Guard. It was clever of you to pick that up, though. Cyrus must be right about you."

"How so?"

"He took one look at you and told me that you were ex-military and probably Special Forces. Was he right?"

Alex considered a moment, then decided he could gain nothing by a lie and lose nothing else with the truth. "Yes."

Yusef nodded. "That makes sense. You are far more clever than any Air Marshals I've encountered before."

"You've done this before?"

"No, but I've flown many times to gauge the effectiveness of the Air Marshals in preparation for this mission."

"How long have you been planning this?"

Yusef chuckled. "Five months. You can get a lot of flying done in five months."

That really wasn't much time to plan and execute a hijacking and kidnapping of an airplane. Of course, the people who had hired Yusef and his crew had likely been planning this for much longer.

Alex debated leaving it at that but decided to try once more to arrange for a peaceful ending to this scenario. "You understand that the United States is going to respond very harshly to this."

"Only if we slaughter you wholesale. The United States is, as you know, very pragmatic. The current regime is reluctant to plunge the nation into another unpopular war like the forays into Iraq and Afghanistan. There will be those in your government who will clamor for our blood, but most of the populace will be against escalation and will encourage your leaders to cooperate and avoid further bloodshed."

"Not with American citizens already dead."

"Of course, with American citizens already dead. Have you thought to wonder why Iran has never actually attacked Israel? Why we have not followed through on our threats to Saudi Arabia? Certainly, many if not most in our government would love to begin the great holy war they preach so fondly about. But the thing about leadership is that you only have it as long as people would rather endure you than die. Once they believe that enduring you will kill more of them than overthrowing you, your reign is over. If we go to war, the people of Iran will believe that enduring the Ayatollah will kill more of them than overthrowing him. So we speak of war, but actions like this are the closest we'll ever come. Your nation threatens retaliation, but short of another 9/11, threats are the closest you'll come."

"You're very confident in that," Alex said. "What if you're wrong?"

"Then, within three months, the Iranian military will be utterly defeated, and a puppet government will be installed in place of the current regime. Over the next ten to fifteen years, that puppet government will be assaulted on all sides with accusations of corruption. American forces will be harassed by insurgents and each death—insignificant though it may be in terms of affecting your military might—will be an uproar in your nation. Over time, the righteous anger that fueled the initial war will be forgotten, and people will just want it to end. They will call for the U.S. to stop meddling and bring their loved ones home. Meanwhile, ultra-nationalists in Iran will drum up support, and the populace—who will have also forgotten the terror of the Ayatollah for anger at the foreign invaders—will flock to their flag. The U.S. will leave, and the new government will look much like the Ayatollah's. And once more, Western thinkers will scratch their heads and wonder why the hell the whole world doesn't share the same values as their own culture."

Alex didn't have a response to that. Yusef smiled at him after a moment, then said, "Let's be honest. We're going to land at the airport, my employers will negotiate whatever it is they want to negotiate and make whatever point they want to make. You and your fellows will undergo perhaps a few weeks of fear and discomfort. Then you will be returned home. You will all make thousands conducting exclusive interviews and offering platitudes of how your strength, your faith in God, your love for your family, or your admiration of some motivational symbol on social media got you through the worst trauma of your privileged, first-world lives. Then, after a few years, you will all forget and go back to being spoiled, selfish people. Just like you always were."

He stood and nodded at Alex. "Enjoy the flight, Air Marshal. Don't beat yourself up over this. It is only temporary."

He left the relief cabin and closed the door.

Alex didn't waste any time digesting Yusef's monologue. He didn't really give a damn if Yusef was wrong or right about the passengers. Killing innocent people was wrong. Period. He didn't need to have an existential crisis about whether or not a lack of cultural understanding was somehow the real culprit behind all this.

Instead, he got straight to work unlocking the panel that would give him contact to the ground and his best chance yet of giving this a happy ending. They had taken his gun and his knife, but they hadn't taken his phone. That was good luck. These terrorists were good, but not great. Alex was in a bad spot, but not nearly as bad as Yusef thought he was.

He turned and just managed to get his fingertips on the latch. His shoulders screamed at him, but he had dealt with far worse pain before.

He unlatched the panel, pulling it open to reveal a small screen with a keyboard underneath. He looked over his shoulder, craning his neck so he could see what he was doing. He carefully pressed the power button. The screen booted up and after a brief welcome message, a menu popped up, written in plain English with options such as NAV, COMM, SYS and SOS.

He was so glad this was a civilian system. The idea of a control panel that wasn't password protected would be unheard of in the military.

He put his finger over the SOS button, but hesitated. If the SOS button released any kind of alarm in the cockpit, then his cover would be blown, and his last best chance of a happy ending to this would be gone.

Instead, he pressed COMM. A second menu opened with three options: INTER, RADIO AND SATT. He pressed SATT, and the screen read DISABLED. Directly underneath that, smaller font asked ENABLE? Y/N.

"Why yes, please," he said softly.

He pressed Y, and a loading screen popped up. He waited for about one minute before the screen read ENABLED.

He grinned and carefully closed the panel, taking care to do so quietly so the noise didn't alert anyone. Now, he needed to get his phone out of his pocket.

That turned out to be trickier than re-engaging the satellite. His phone was in his front pocket, and his hands were bound tightly to his back and from there to the padlock of the cockpit luggage hold. How ironic that they would have a padlock for the luggage hold but allow anyone who was curious access to the airplane's critical systems.

He had to twist his body almost to the point of dislocating his right shoulder, but he finally managed to remove the phone. For a terrifying split second, he nearly dropped it in between the bench on which he sat and the bulkhead, but he slammed his hand over it and pulled it onto the seat safely just before it fell out of reach.

He breathed a sigh of relief and opened the phone. Once more, it was tricky to unlock the phone and type on the tiny screen, but he managed to get the messaging app open. A second later, thirteen messages loaded. The first was a response to his text about Iran. *Pat in contact with Washington. Will contact Iranian government.* The next four were updates on the situation ending with the fifth that told him the Iranian government was denying everything, of course.

The next message was when Sarah realized they had lost contact with the airplane. The final six messages occurred at intervals of fifteen minutes as she checked to see if contact had been reestablished.

Alex wondered if it was a good thing or a bad thing that the Iranian government knew they were onto them. Probably a very bad thing for Yusef and his crew, but he wasn't sure what that would mean for the hostages.

He texted Sarah. *Comms back. Terrorists have plane. Destination Bandar Abbas. I am bound in relief cabin. Six casualties, four passengers and two crew. One terrorist down. Five remaining. Leader is ex Revolutionary Guard. Name given is Yusef, possibly false. Other names given include Bashir, Mahmoud, Cryus, Hasam and the deceased, Abdul. Cyrus almost certainly ex-military as well. The other three civilians.*

He sent that text to prevent the lag that would occur with a large message, then composed another. *Goals unclear. Terrorists are reluctant to use violence except to retain control of the aircraft. Hasam has medical experience. They definitely want us alive. Who exactly "they" are or what they want with us, I'm not sure.*

Sarah, the consummate professional, saved exclamations of joy that he was still alive and also saved exclamations of fear at the danger they were still in. She only replied *Status of aircraft?*

He sent back, *Captain and first officer attempted crash landing, believing Burj Khalifa to be target. Relief crew piloting now. Navigation and GPS tracking down. Radio down. Believe satellite transponder is the only active system now besides minimum flight systems. Maneuvering has reduced range by perhaps seven hundred fifty miles. Still more than enough fuel to divert if they decide they need to.*

A minute later, Sarah replied. *Understood. Iran continues to deny. Pat says do not provoke a massacre. Take aircraft only if possible without bloodshed. I say I know you can do it, so good luck, be safe and let me know when it's done.*

Alex smiled. Just being able to talk to Sarah had improved his mood considerably. *Will do,* he replied.

Then he put his phone back in his pocket, a task nearly as difficult as taking it out. Then he settled back and considered his next steps.

But he didn't rush. He had his resources now. He would do things right this time. This time, he wouldn't make mistakes.

CHAPTER FOURTEEN

This was not what Mahmoud expected. Hell, he might as well come out and admit it. This was going badly.

When he envisioned this job, he envisioned a plane full of cowardly, meek passengers timidly following his every instruction. He imagined himself and his fellow hijackers intimidating people to the point where no one would dare so much as look at him, let alone complain to him, let alone actively defy him and even attack two of his men.

He certainly never imagined that an Air Marshal would incite disobedience to the point of rioting, or that the pilots would get an attack of courage and give that Air Marshal a chance to kill Abdul and take his weapon.

He imagined himself earning Yusef's praise and perhaps receiving permission to lead a job of his own in the future. Now, he would be lucky to have employment after this. It wouldn't surprise him at all if Yusef handed him his paycheck and told him to fuck off and stay there.

"At least he'll pay me," he muttered under his breath.

"What?" a passenger in the front seat quacked.

He cast the dumpling shaped woman a contemptuous sneer and said, "I wasn't talking to you. Be quiet."

The woman actually had the audacity to huff, offended by his attitude. He felt an urge to slap her with the barrel of his machine pistol and ask if she'd like to feel it rammed up her snout, but he controlled himself. He wasn't Bashir.

Bashir. Mahmoud glanced at his comrade and found him glaring at one of the pockets of passengers who actually behaved the way they were supposed to, cowering in fear and not daring to do or say anything to raise the ire of the terrorists.

He hadn't known Bashir long, but his past experience with the older man suggested to him that Bashir would be calm and collected under pressure, that he would show the wisdom of one his age and conduct himself more like Hasan or Cyrus.

Instead, he acted like a pup with no self-control and picked on the weak to stroke what was clearly a horrifically fragile ego.

It was his fault they were in this position. He couldn't comprehend the need to be quiet and unassuming. Several times, he went to speak to Mahmoud, clarifying mundane points of the operation that they had gone over several times before.

"So we're going to take all three cabins and the cockpit at the same time, right?"

"Yes, Bashir."

"We want to turn south, then disable satellite tracking before turning east again, right?"

"Yes, but that's not your job. Don't worry about it."

"We're going to drop the plane off at Bander Abbas, then leave immediately after turning it over to the Revolutionary Guard, right?"

"Bashir, stop talking to me. That man in 30C has been staring at you the past ten minutes."

Then they take the plane and Bashir turns into some sort of psychopath. Yusef had been very clear. We remain in command, but we don't lose control. We intimidate them by being in flawless command of our emotions, not by being aggressive.

Bashir didn't get the memo. He started swearing at everyone, waving his gun around like a gangster, spitting and snarling like a madman. What a fool.

Then he had terrorized that mother over her child. Mahmoud felt no sympathy for yet another harlot who carried a bastard child and dressed like she couldn't wait for another man to give her another bastard, but that didn't mean he was foolish enough to single her out.

Bashir caught his eye and offered a sharklike grin. Mahmoud turned away.

Bashir hadn't singled her out. He was just waiting for the chance to use his gun, and she gave it to him. Mahmoud could almost smell the disappointment when Mahmoud shot that old man before Bashir could.

That old man would never have left his seat if Bashir had just let that little boy use the bathroom. He would never have reached for Bashir's gun, and Mahmoud wouldn't have had to shoot him. The Air Marshal would have remained in his chair, choosing to act in the best way to protect his charges.

That was what grated on him the most. They had assured the passengers that they would be kept alive. True, that was conditioned on their good behavior, but they wanted to keep everyone unharmed. If they had, then the Air Marshal would have believed that caution was the best way to act. Instead, they had shown that they would kill passengers, and the Air Marshal had to find a way to take the plane from them.

And it had gone downhill from there. The Air Marshal had pushed and found their weakness. They would only kill passengers if absolutely necessary. He had made them show their hand, and then he had exploited that. He had found a way to get to the restroom, probably to contact someone back home, then—

Oh shit.

"Bashir. Watch coach. I need to speak to Yusef."

He spoke in Farsi, and Bashir managed to remember to reply in the same language. "What about?"

About how we should kill you and toss your worthless corpse out of the nearest door, you worthless waste. Would Allah it had been you instead of Abdul.

"Just watch coach."

Bashir frowned. "Why are you so rude to me?"

"You want to talk about this now?" he hissed.

Bashir's frown turned into a sulk, which Mahmoud didn't stay to witness. He stomped irritably to first class. Hasam noticed his expression and frowned. Mahmoud waved his hand to let Hasam know it was nothing serious—a lie, but he needed to talk to Yusef before anyone else knew what he was thinking.

It galled him that Yusef blamed him for the situation in coach. It wasn't his fault. Bashir wouldn't listen to him. He was the reason everything had gone to crap. Warning Yusef about the fact that the Air Marshal had probably contacted the Air Force would show Yusef that he was still useful. It would likely be years before he got the chance to run his own job, but at least he would *have* a job.

Yusef stood at the head of first class, watching over a flock of meek little lambs. The man was a *daeva*. It was incredible how effortlessly he bent things to his will with no more effort than it took Mahmoud to button his shirt.

He looked at Mahmoud, and Mahmoud gestured that he needed to speak to him. Yusef frowned slightly but didn't refuse. He turned to the sheep and said, "I must speak with my colleague for a moment. Remain seated."

They stepped close to the relief cabin and spoke in Farsi in low voices.

"The Air Marshal contacted someone," Mahmoud said.

Yusef raised an eyebrow. "You know this for sure?"

"I am almost certain. He went to the lavatory under a ruse before the pilots tried to crash the plane. I believe he was trying to contact someone."

Yusef sighed. "He failed."

"He…" Mahmoud blinked. "Failed?"

"When we disabled satellite tracking, we also severed satellite and radio communications. Even if he had a handheld device, he would be unable to connect to a satellite without the airplane's hull scrambling the signal, and he would have to be within fifty miles of a transceiver to send a radio signal. I appreciate you coming to me with this, Mahmoud, but there is nothing to worry about."

"Oh," Mahmoud was crushed. This was his way to prove his usefulness. Instead, he looked foolish.

"Is Amal still concealed?" Yusef asked.

"Yes," Mahmoud said, recovering. "He is in his seat behaving like a frightened passenger."

"Good. We need one man to be unrevealed in case of any more unforeseen circumstances. I don't believe these passengers will attempt to take the plane, but if anyone does, it will be coach."

Due to your mismanagement, Yusef didn't say but Mahmoud heard as clearly as though he had.

"If that happens," Yusef continued, "Amal's presence may cut that off before it goes too far."

The fact that he was explaining this made it clear that he didn't value Mahmoud's intelligence. It was obvious that having a hidden man was beneficial. Yet Yusef felt a need to make that clear.

He fought desperately to think of something he could say that would demonstrate his relevance. "What of the Air Marshal? Will we keep him alive?"

"Yes. For now."

Mahmoud blinked. This genuinely did surprise him. "Really? But he killed Abdul!"

"It was your choice to allow him to use the restroom at the front of the cabin combined with the pilot's choice to sacrifice this airplane that gave him the opportunity."

Mahmoud felt as though a knife had been run through his chest. At the same time, anger flared. "That was *not* my fault!"

"Of course not," Yusef said calmly. "You couldn't have known the pilots would do what they did. Had the Air Marshal entered business class without a distraction, Abdul would have discovered him and probably killed him. It was an unfortunate and unforeseen circumstance that led to Abdul's death. Still, you should have had him use the rear restroom."

Mahmoud's cheeks burned with shame and anger, but Yusef was right. He had made a grave error by allowing the Air Marshal anywhere near business class, and he had paid for it.

Abdul had paid for it.

His anger faded, and he lowered his head.

"Don't let your emotions cloud you. Learn from this. As for the Air Marshal, he is an employee of the United States Federal Government. He will be useful to the Revolutionary Guard when the time comes to negotiate. He will know how to talk to his people to ensure that their results are maximized."

"He will also know how to sabotage them."

"He won't sabotage them. He is charged with protecting these passengers. He will do what will keep most of them alive the longest. That means cooperating, not resisting."

Mahmoud sighed. "I worry, though. I don't claim that I'm not to blame in part for Abdul's death, but he is smart, Yusef. Even you didn't know he was here." He quickly added, "Granted, you weren't in coach, but—"

"No, you're right," Yusef said. "He fooled all of us. He is a dangerous foe."

Mahmoud felt a leap of joy at being told by Yusef that he was right. It occurred to him that in many ways, he considered Yusef a father. He wondered if it was healthy to hang on his every word this way.

He didn't wonder for long, though. Feeling proud of himself was better than feeling irritated, guilty and afraid. "I think it would be safer to kill him, Yusef."

"No. He can be useful. He is tied somewhere he cannot escape from. He won't be any more trouble."

Mahmoud sighed. "I hope you're right."

"I am. Trust me." He laid a hand on the younger man's shoulder. "You are young and passionate, Mahmoud. This is good. Don't lose that passion. But allow wisdom to temper it. The only difference between passion and fear is looking over one's left shoulder rather than one's right."

Mahmoud nodded. "I will, Yusef."

Yusef smiled and clapped him on the shoulder. "Good man. Return to your post. Don't worry about the Air Marshal. I can handle him. I know how he thinks."

"Of course, Yusef."

Mahmoud returned to Coach, feeling a little better about things. He still worried that the Air Marshal was more dangerous than Yusef believed, but he also believed that no matter how dangerous he was, Yusef was more dangerous.

They would still succeed.

CHAPTER FIFTEEN

Alex's phone buzzed, but he didn't reach for it this time. He would check it in a few minutes, but right now, he was moments away from releasing one of the knots that bound him to the padlock on the cockpit luggage hold. That would allow him considerably more movement and make undoing the rest of his bonds much easier.

He focused on controlling his breathing and maintaining stillness in his body. His upper body was twisted, his abs and shoulders straining to hold the twist against the pressure exerted by his bonds. His ankles and wrists were tied together in such a way that it was difficult for him to engage his lower back muscles to aid him. He could already feel a burning at the base of his spine that would turn into painful swelling in the next couple of days.

All things considered, that was pretty low on the list of worries.

He was almost there. Just an inch more. Just an inch—

His right heel slipped on the floor. Just barely, maybe a millimeter, but the release of kinetic energy caused the rest of the rope to contract, and his hands were pulled painfully up and to the left. He struggled against it right up to the point where continuing to resist would result in his shoulder being dislocated, then sighed and allowed his body to relax.

Pain shot through his body, but it paled in comparison to his disappointment.

"Damn it."

He shook his head and considered trying again, but he couldn't do it right away. He needed to allow his muscles to relax for a minute or two, or he risked spasms. If he got spasms, he could potentially make releasing his bonds impossible.

God, he hated getting old. He was in great shape, outstanding shape for an Air Marshal and probably still good enough to pass BUD/s without too much trouble, but he wasn't quite the twenty-five-year-old monster he was when he first pinned on his Trident. Damage lingered just a bit longer than it did when he was younger, and recovery took just a bit longer.

Once more, Old Joe Lincoln's voice sounded in his mind. *Bitching is for soldiers and airmen. You're a fucking Frogman. Suck it up.*

He had to smile at that. Old Joe wasn't shy about airing his opinion of training standards in the other branches.

"Got any advice for how to get my ass out of a damn Houdini rope trap, Joe?"

Old Joe didn't.

He sighed and decided to check his messages while he was waiting. Now that he knew what to do, getting the phone out of his pocket wasn't as hard as before. When he pulled the phone out, he opened it up and checked Sarah's message.

CIA reaching out to assets in Revolutionary Guard. Possible intel transfer.

Alex frowned. Intel transfer? That meant that someone on this plane was giving information to the Revolutionary Guard. They were probably disguising it as a ransom, but if she was right, the true purpose was espionage.

He wondered if the terrorists were all aware that they were transporting a spy. Yusef probably was, but he might not have been told who the spy was. That was probably why they had been ordered not to kill passengers. Their employers didn't want to risk that their asset would be harmed before he or she could deliver information.

He texted back. *Give CIA roster. Tell them the passengers were clean for us. They might have info we don't.*

A moment later, he received a text. *Who do you think you're talking to? Already done,* mijo.

He smiled. It was nice that Sarah believed in him so much that the thought of him getting killed never even crossed her mind.

It had crossed his. It didn't really bother him. To be honest, he felt like he was overdue for his meeting with the ferry to Tartarus. He was the only person who survived a crash that killed everyone else in his team, and he came home whole from a war that hadn't even spared his civilian brother.

That was the first time he had thought of Ben for the first time since this ordeal began. He felt a pang of guilt about that. It was true that he had a job to focus on and couldn't take time to feel sorry for himself, but to not even spare a thought for his only living family member hours deep into a terrorist operation that could end in his death?

Maybe Ben was right. Maybe the part of him that could love really was broken. Maybe that was why dating was a non-starter for him.

That brought up an image of Emma, but he pushed that thought away. He wasn't going to think of a woman he was attracted to when he had only just thought about his brother. Instead, his mind drifted back to a conversation he and Ben had when Alex was home on leave for a few weeks before heading to BUD/s.

"So you're going to be a SEAL now. Damn, you've gone native, bro. What happened to driving submarines?"

Alex chuckled. "Well, I was applying for the school when I looked up and saw these badasses carrying logs and boats and running backwards uphill with bags of rocks tied to their shoulders."

"So you got into the SEALs by staring at men. Good to know. I know some hot guys if you want me to set you up."

"Yeah, but you should see what these guys do in the water."

Ben laughed at that. "You realize you're going to have to swim, right? A lot."

Alex had never been a fan of swimming. He'd preferred dry land sports. One of his favorite phrases growing up was, "If I were meant to be a fish, I would have been born with fins." He shrugged. "I guess I'll learn."

Ben shook his head. "I'll never understand you, dude."

That was one of Alex's last good memories of Ben.

He took a breath and got back to work on the ropes. This time, he pushed himself up as far as he could and used his left foot to brace himself against the bulkhead. This gave him more leverage to twist and gain access to the loop of cord he was trying to release.

Unfortunately, it also tightened the cord to the point that he was unable to undo it. He grabbed hold of it and tried to hold on as he relaxed and lowered himself back to a seating position, but it was made of some sort of synthetic material that slid easily off of his skin. The cord slipped through his fingers, and two attempts to do the same thing resulted in similar failure.

When he felt his back threaten to spasm again, he sighed in frustration and relaxed. This wasn't going to work. He had to think of another way.

Maybe he could use brute force. The ropes were far beyond his ability to tear, and the padlock was the sort that could only be cut by a diamond bladed power saw, but the hinges on the luggage hold doors were standard locker room aluminum sheet fasteners. If he could tear the doors off, he could get his body at a better angle to undo the knots.

Doing that would make a lot more noise too, however. The sound of the doors ripping free and then clanging all over the bulkhead would no doubt attract attention. He could always hope that some other unforeseen event would give him the chance, but he knew better than to rely on continued miracles.

He wrestled with the decision for a while before finally deciding the attempt wasn't worth it. If they caught him before he could get free—and odds were that they would—they would either kill him or learn their lesson and bind him differently and to a much stronger anchor. It would be a waste of time.

Or maybe he could pull it free slowly. If he could pull it enough to strip the fasteners but not enough to tear them out, he could gently pull the door out little by little until it came free. The risk of noise would be much less that way. Then, the only risk would be time. It would take several minutes to remove the door and another several minutes to remove the bonds. During that time, he would be vulnerable.

But the terrorists had a plane to watch, and no one had come to check on him in the two hours he'd been locked here. He was pretty sure he could do it if—"

He heard the sound of the door to the relief cabin opening and stifled a curse. *Of course someone has to come check on me now that I think about it.*

He sat back against the wall and waited.

The door opened, but it wasn't one of the terrorists who walked into the room. Alex's eyes widened in shock when Emma carefully stepped in and closed the door.

"Emma?" he whispered. "What are you doing here? How did you get here?"

"Rescuing you," she replied, "and carefully. The terrorists are talking in the galley. I think they're arguing over what to do when they land the plane. I heard Yusef telling the others to worry about the job and let the employers worry about the rest. It sounds like the two younger ones don't agree."

"If they catch you, they'll kill you."

"I don't think so. I think they'll just tie me up. But let's hurry anyway."

She reached behind Alex and began working the knots loose. He caught a scent of almonds and vanilla in her hair, and a thrill ran through his body. He allowed himself a moment to be amazed and annoyed that he could think of that at a time like this, then refocused on the matter at hand.

She got him loose and pumped her fist in excitement. "What now?" she asked him eagerly.

Alex thought a moment, then said, "I'm going to hand you my cell phone. The top contact is Sarah Castillo. That's my partner. She's working from the ground to help us once the plane touches down. I want you to monitor texts from her and tell her any major developments on board."

She blinked. "What? But I don't know anything important."

"It doesn't matter. Tell her everything, and she'll determine what's important and what isn't."

"What will you do?"

"I'm going to try to take the plane. Part of your job will be to tell Sarah if I fail."

Emma frowned. "I didn't release you so you could get hurt doing something stupid."

"I have to do something. If we end up in Iranian custody, we're not long for this world."

"So they were lying."

She didn't seem very surprised. "I don't know if they're lying or if they honestly don't know. These guys are PMCs."

"PMCs?"

"Private Military Contractors. Guns for hire. They got told to take this airplane and keep the passengers alive." He paused a moment while considering what to tell her. In the end, he decided to keep out the part about the possible spy and only told her the crucial conclusion. "I think that they want something or someone on this plane, and once they have that something or someone, the rest of us will be expendable."

"They can't kill us! The United States will go to war!"

Alex smiled bitterly. "Maybe, but I doubt it. Besides, the Iranian government has been getting more volatile with each passing year. Maybe this is when they finally decide that war is worth the risk."

"They can't be that foolish."

"Fanaticism makes fools out of a lot of people."

"But…" her voice trailed off as his point sank in.

"That's why I need to take this plane. We can't land in Iran."

Emma nodded understanding. Then she met Alex's eyes. There was a great deal of fear in her expression, but there was also resolve. "Do what you have to do, Alex."

Hearing his name roll off her lips was like a breath of fresh air. "I will. Go back to coach now. If they catch you up here, the whole thing goes off the rails."

She nodded once more, then left the relief cabin. Alex counted to sixty, then got up to leave himself.

Then he paused. A better idea occurred to him.

If he took the cockpit, he would have the plane. If he took the cockpit and somehow kept that fact hidden from the terrorists, then he could take away the threat of landing in Iran and take a lot of pressure off of himself to handle this quickly.

He carefully closed the door to the cabin and positioned himself in front of the door to the cockpit.

CHAPTER SIXTEEN

Alex paused a moment before knocking. He would have to take Cyrus out quickly and quietly, just as he had Abdul. Aside from the risk of calling the other terrorists, if either of them bumped into the wrong button, he had no idea what could happen to the aircraft.

He switched to the side of the door where the hinges were so he would have a half-second of concealment when Cyrus opened the door. He couldn't count on more than that half-second. Cyrus didn't give Alex the impression of being as skilled as Yusef, but he did have military experience, and when he heard a knock and opened the door to see nothing there, he would put two and two together very quickly. Alex needed to make sure he didn't get that chance.

He readied himself, then knocked on the door.

Cyrus called in Farsi, and Alex's heart sank. Of course, Yusef would have agreed on some sort of catchphrase or passcode. Now, he had alerted them to his plan.

Don't give them too much credit, Old Joe's voice said in his mind. *Giving an enemy too much credit is as bad as not giving them enough.*

Boy, I hope you're right about that, Joe, he thought.

He knocked on the door again. Once more, Cyrus called in Farsi.

But then Alex saw the handle drop as Cyrus opened the door. He waited until the terrorist stepped past the door, then lunged. Cyrus saw him just in time to open his mouth.

Alex grabbed his neck and twisted hard. The big man dropped like a rock, and Alex caught him and dragged him into the cockpit.

The relief pilots stared at him in shock. The copilot's face lit up with joy, and she opened her mouth to exclaim, but Alex quickly shook his head and brought a finger to his lips.

She clammed up, and he said, "Close the door."

The copilot hesitated a moment. Then his command clicked in her head, and she quickly unbuckled and jumped off of her chair.

Alex laid Cyrus's body against the bulkhead after the copilot closed and locked the door. He took the terrorist's weapon, then turned to the pilots and said, "Okay, let's talk about how to get ourselves out of this."

"What do you mean?" the pilot asked. "We're not out?"

"No. There are still four more terrorists. They don't know that I'm here."

The pilot deflated a little. "Oh. Well, shouldn't you be going after them?"

"Yes, but not right this second. Right now, they need to think the cockpit is still under their control. So don't alter course just yet. The plan at the moment is for you guys to land in Dubai, but I'm going to see if we can upgrade that to a Saudi airbase. Where is your satellite communications?"

"We don't have them. They're shut down."

"Not anymore. I rebooted them using the backup terminal."

The pilot's eyes widened. "Hell yeah!"

Fortunately, he remembered to keep his exclamation quiet.

"We can celebrate later," Alex said. "They'll figure out I'm here eventually. I need to get a message to my friends before then."

The pilot pressed a couple of buttons, then handed him the headset. "You use this knob to set the channel, then just use it like a normal radio."

Alex took a moment to recall the TSA New York office's satellite channel, then dialed.

A voice answered, "TSA New York, who is this?"

"This is Air Marshal Alex Hawkins. I need to speak to Air Marshal Sarah Castillo immediately."

"Oh, shit. Hey, Sarah! I have Alex on the line!"

A moment later, Alex heard Sarah's voice. "Alex? How did you get the radio working? Do you have the plane?"

"Not yet, but I have the cockpit. Listen, I want to put us down before we get to Bandar Abbas. I'm not convinced the Iranians will let us go once they have the asset they want. Can you call the Saudi government and see if they'll let us use one of their airfields on the Persian Gulf?"

A second familiar voice replied to that. "I'll put it through the proper channels. I should have an answer for you in ten minutes. Can you stay on the line?"

"I'm not sure, ma'am. The terrorists still think I'm in captivity. I'm locked in the cockpit right now, but if they start threatening to shoot people unless I open up, I'm going to be between a rock and a hard place."

Supervisory Air Marshal in Charge Patricia Bennett was fifteen years older than Alex but retained the vigor of a much younger woman.

That, combined with a mind as sharp as any Alex had ever known, made her the most decorated Air Marshal in the Service's history. That distinction was relative since an Air Marshal's job was to make sure that terrorist attacks and hijackings were stopped before anyone had a chance to hear about them, but within the Service, at least, she occupied a pedestal that few Marshals in the Service's history shared.

"Understood, Alex. I'll move as quickly as I can. If I were you, I would plan on landing at Abdulaziz."

Alex's eyes widened. "You want me to land at a major Saudi Air Base?"

"They won't be happy about an unauthorized landing, but I'd bet that landing will become authorized, either before you land or retroactively. They're our allies, and even if they don't love us, per se, they need our support to remain in power. They're not going to put a plane full of American civilians in danger. You'll be in for a few uncomfortable hours getting led away in blindfolds, but when those blindfolds come off, you'll be in U.S. custody.

"And that's a worst-case scenario. Odds are, once we tell them we're doing this to foil an Iranian op, they'll be falling all over themselves to take credit and stick it to their neighbors across the pond."

"Can you use across the pond for the Persian Gulf?"

"I just did. Tell your pilots to head there, surreptitiously, if they can, and plan on that being where you land."

"Will do. Thank you—"

There was a knock at the cockpit door, followed by Yusef's voice speaking Farsi.

Alex closed the connection and handed the headset back to the pilot. He drew the pistol and approached the door slowly.

There was another knock, and Yusef called more urgently. When Alex didn't reply, Yusef said, "Okay, Alex. It looks like you've defeated Cyrus. Good job. I'm not sure how you managed to slip your bonds, but clearly I've underestimated you."

"It's over now, Yusef. I have the aircraft. I'm putting us down at King Abdulaziz Air Base in Saudi Arabia. If you and your friends want a chance of surviving this, you need to surrender now and allow yourselves to be detained."

"And how many of your passengers are you willing to risk to do that?"

"How much are you willing to risk? Your employers made it clear that they wanted every single one of these passengers safe if possible.

They want us all alive when we land. Do you really think they'll be pleased if they find out you killed dozens of them just to win a pissing match with us?"

"I think they'll be far angrier if the plane lands in Saudi Arabia."

"So I guess it's how much I'm willing to lose versus how much you're willing to lose."

"I'll take that bet. Mahmoud, bring Emma here."

Alex resisted the urge to give up immediately and ensure Emma's safety. He knew he was grabbing at the thinnest of straws right now, but he wasn't willing to let it go just yet.

"Here's the thing: I'm willing to bet you know more than you're telling your subordinates. I think you know the real reason your government wants this plane. I think you *don't* know *who* they want. And your government clearly doesn't want to tell you. For all you know, that person might already be dead."

"In which case, there's no point in refraining from slaughtering everyone."

Damn it. "On the other hand, if that person *is* alive, and you kill them trying to beat me, then you'll be landing this prize with great fanfare that will last exactly as long as it takes the Revolutionary Guard to realize you fucked up. You have more experience with them than I do, so you tell me: what happens to you in that scenario?"

This pause was far longer than the others. When Yusef spoke again, Alex detected the first crack in his façade. "You're bluffing."

"So are you. Like I said, it comes down to who's willing to risk the most."

"Bashir. There is an asset on board this plane. Find out who it is and sequester them. Once you've done that, kill the woman. Make it last a long time so the Air Marshal can hear her scream."

"This plane is landing in Saudi Arabia," Alex said. "You can kill passengers if you want, but each passenger you kill increases the likelihood of severe consequences against your government."

"The United States will not go to war over one aircraft. They will use you as a scapegoat and claim it is your incompetence that resulted in these innocents' deaths."

My thoughts exactly. Let's hope you're bluffing.

"Open the door and end this nonsense," Yusef continued. "You are a professional. Act like one and accept defeat graciously."

"That's not how Americans work."

"Spare me the nationalist nonsense. Bashir, have you found the asset?"

"I've found him, sir."

"Wonderful. Kill the girl."

Alex braced himself. If he was wrong, then he had just gotten an innocent killed. If he was right, then he might very likely have saved them all.

There was no sound for over a minute. No gunfire, no screaming, no cries of pain or fear.

Alex smiled. He was right. "You still there, Yusef?" he called brightly.

"I am still here. Well done, Air Marshal. You are right. My superiors will react poorly if I bring them a plane of corpses, and yes, in their infinite wisdom, the leaders of the Revolutionary Guard have declined to inform me of who or what exactly they want. Perhaps they will learn from this failure and better prepare their agents in the future. In the meantime, it appears we are at your mercy. However, I will not simply surrender. I will continue to hold these passengers hostage until safety is granted my men. I will enter U.S. custody, not Saudi custody. Is that clear?"

Alex nodded. "I'm sure that can be worked out. No more killing civilians, though, understand?"

"Of course. As I said, Alex. You win."

Then the door to the cockpit burst open and Bashir and Yusef rushed Alex, guns raised.

CHAPTER SEVENTEEN

Alex threw himself to the side, moving on instinct more than conscious thought. Yusef caught the movement and held his fire, but Bashir fired a burst. One of the bullets caught Alex in the right arm and threw him onto his back.

The other bullets pierced through the copilot's chair and buried themselves in her body. She jerked with each round, then slumped over. The pilot cried out and jerked the yoke to the left, also moving on instinct.

That instinct saved Alex's life. The plane lurched, and Yusef and Bashir fell and slid to the other side of the cockpit.

Alex slid toward them, pressing his heels into the floor to slow the movement. He saw Bashir snarl and aim his weapon at the cockpit.

Yusef shouted in Farsi, probably telling Bashir to stop being an idiot, but he needn't have worried. Alex fired, and the bullet struck Bashir's wrist. He cried out and dropped his weapon.

Yusef aimed at Alex, but the pilot corrected his movement, and the men began to tumble the other way. Yusef fired a short burst, and three bullets slammed into the side of the cockpit.

"Hey!" the pilot shouted. "You blow a hole in here, we all die!"

That wasn't true, but it was a good bluff. The terrorist narrowed his eyes and dropped his weapon. Alex kept his trained on Yusef, holding it in his left hand and getting slowly to his feet. His right arm could move, but it felt weak, and the hand didn't want to close into a fist.

"All right," he said, "You too."

"Hey!"

Alex turned to see Mahmoud rushing toward them, aiming his gun. *Damn it.*

He rushed for the door and kicked it shut just before a spray of bullets left impressions in the thick aluminum bulkhead. He turned back just in time for Yusef to grab his weapon and force him back against the door.

"Bashir!" Yusef called. "The door!"

The younger terrorist rushed for them. Alex tried to push Yusef away, but the terrorist planted his feet and held him in place. Instead, when Bashir approached, Alex brought his foot up in between his legs. Bashir's mouth and eyes popped open in the triple O of surprise that every man knew all too well. Then he dropped to the floor.

Yusef snarled at him in Farsi, but the momentary distraction allowed Alex to plant his right foot and bring his left knee up to the same target on Yusef. Yusef grunted in pain but kept his feet. Still, the blow weakened his leg, and Alex was able to shift his hips and trip him, bringing them both to the ground.

Bashir got to his feet slowly, but Alex kicked at his ankle, tripping him too. The terrorist went down hard, slamming his head onto the cockpit floor with an audible clang. His eyes rolled back in his head, then closed.

Alex felt the gun rip out of his hand and turned around to see Yusef pointing right at him. He lunged for the terrorist, shoving the weapon up just as Yusef fired. A set of holes appeared in the ceiling above them, and Alex heard a whistling sound as pressurized air rushed out of the cockpit.

"Guys!" the pilot shouted, "Are you serious?"

Yeah, a little, Alex thought drily.

Yusef snarled and twisted his body, throwing Alex over his shoulder. He was surprisingly strong for his size, and the unexpected throw once more tore Alex's hands off of the gun.

"I have to descend now," the pilot said in a remarkably petulant tone. "If I don't get us to flight level 125 in the next fifteen minutes, we're all going to pass out from lack of oxygen and end up dead."

Yusef aimed the gun at Alex, but Alex kicked up and knocked it from his hands. Yusef turned toward it, but Alex tackled him and threw him to the ground. He started to position himself above Yusef, but the plane nosed down. He lost balance for a split second, but that split second was enough for Yusef to scoop his leg and throw him over to the other side. Alex hit the ground and tumbled toward the nose.

He looked up and saw Yusef getting to his feet and heading for the door. He quickly scrambled to his and rushed forward.

Yusef turned the handle and began to open the door. Alex slammed into him, throwing both of them into the door. Yusef cried out when his head hit the door, but unlike Bashir, he didn't fall unconscious.

Alex reached for the handle, but then Mahmoud hit the door, pushing him back. He just managed to keep his feet and hold the door just open, not enough for Mahmoud to sneak through.

Mahmoud shouted in Farsi, and Yusef shouted back. Alex brought his leg ahead of Yusef's, but the terrorist simply dropped behind Alex and wrapped his hands around his waist. Alex instantly spread his legs and dropped his weight, pressing into the door and keeping Yusef from throwing him.

He struggled with all of his might, and for several seconds, the three of them remained in a stalemate. One on one, Alex would have handled either of them, but with an injured arm against both of them, he was barely able to meet their strength.

Then Mahmoud called, "Hasam!" and Alex knew he had no time left. He allowed Yusef to pull him back a few inches, enough so that the door began to open.

Then with a roar, he threw himself at the door. He heard the satisfying clang as the door impacted Mahmoud's head, then the infinitely more satisfying clang as the door closed.

Yusef snarled with rage, then, with another shocking burst of strength, fell backwards and threw Alex over his shoulder. Alex just managed to cover his head before he crashed into Bashir's head. The other terrorist jerked and spasmed when his head once more hit the hard aluminum floor of the plane, and Alex knew that he was dead this time.

Yusef stared at what he had done in shock. "Bashir!"

Alex took advantage of this momentary distraction to drive his knee into Yusef's jaw. Yusef cried out and flew backwards, and Alex threw a spinning back kick that caught Yusef in the ribs. Alex heard a crack, and the terrorist gasped and clutched his left side as he skidded across the ground toward the wall.

"Will you guys stop this shit?" the pilot shouted, struggling to keep the lurching plane under control. Sparks flew from control panels, and each blow jostled one or both men against the pilot, causing the yoke to bump and twist yet again. "You're going to break something, and we're *all* going to die! Why do I have to keep saying this?"

Yusef looked at Alex, and Alex approached cautiously, ready to deliver the killing blow. Yusef feinted toward Alex's left, then pivoted and sprinted to his right. Alex lunged, but his right arm wouldn't work right. His open hand slapped across Yusef's face without grabbing him.

If he'd had more room, he could have stopped Yusef, but in the close confines of the cockpit, he could only watch Yusef—in a final act of rage and hate–snapped the pilot's neck.

He stared in disbelief as the pilot slumped over, knocking the yoke to the left. The plane banked again, and Alex lunged for the yoke, leveling the aircraft out. His eyes hunted for the trim tab, but before he could find it, he felt a searing pain as something slid into his ribs. He gasped and turned to see the knife—his knife—rushing toward him again.

He caught it and twisted Yusef's wrist, knocking the knife free. It slid under the control panel, and when Yusef's eyes followed it, Alex grabbed the back of his head and drove his knee upward.

Yusef brought both hands up to catch the knee. It kept him from being knocked unconscious but didn't keep him from being thrown backward. Alex held him back with one hand and leveled the plane again just before it banked too far to the right.

The shift in weight caused him to lose his balance. Yusef grabbed his ankle, and Alex managed to pull his foot away before Yusef wrenched it, but he ended up crashing into the opposite wall. His elbow slid over a bunch of toggles, and warning lights flashed in the cabin.

Hope that's not too important, he thought.

Yusef lunged forward and shoved the yoke all the way back. The jet nosed down sharply, and Alex cried out and grabbed at it.

Yusef pushed off of the control panel and shoved Alex to the back wall. "You want to die so badly?" he shouted at Alex. "Then die!"

The self-control and poise he had shown earlier was gone now. In its place was a snarling, raging animal that thought of nothing other than killing as much as it could. Just like Mahmoud, it had all been a veneer, just a slightly thicker one in his case.

Alex struggled against him, but his wounds were weakening him, and his blood soaked both of their bodies and the floor underneath him, making it hard for him to get purchase. Yusef snarled with a strength born of rage and held him against the wall.

Alex realized he wasn't going to overpower him, so he tried reasoning with the terrorist instead. "What about your mission, Yusef? What about Mahmoud and Hasam?"

"They knew the risks! If I let you live, then I compromise my mission!"

Alex heard the groan of the airframe as the plane picked up speed. He looked through the windscreen at the rapidly approaching ground.

A chime sounded, and a clinical female voice announced that they were approaching critical airspeed. A moment later, another chime sounded, and the same voice informed them that their altitude had dropped below twenty thousand feet.

"One hundred feet! Oh, fuck, oh fuck, oh fuck, oh fuck, oh FUCK!"

"Okay. I'll stop resisting. Level out the plane."

"You die first," Yusef said. "Then I'll take the plane and get us back where we're supposed to go."

He snarled and jammed his finger into the knife wound in Alex's side. Pain rolled through him in nauseating waves. He tried to push Yusef away with his left hand, but Yusef caught his wrist and slammed it against the wall. He snarled and pushed his finger in deeper.

"It wasn't your fault, Alex. There was nothing you could do. The helicopter was going down."

His mother's voice threatened to bring Alex the comfort of surrender, but Old Joe's voice intervened.

"Fuck that! You're a goddamned Frogman, and there are lives depending on you! Grab your nuts and stop this!"

Alex brought his head back, then with a cry, slammed it onto Yusef's nose. The blow wasn't particularly strong with none of his body weight behind it, but the nose bone was a very fragile one, while the forehead was the strongest part of the skull. Yusef's nose shattered, and as pain and shock strobed through his face, he forgot what he was doing and let Alex go.

And Alex hit him hard. The blow sent him crashing to the floor, and Alex lifted his boot and brought it down hard on Yusef's head over and over and over and over again.

He didn't stop until the flight computer announced that they had dropped below ten thousand feet.

His head snapped back to the windshield. The ground rushed at him with sickening speed.

He had less than ten seconds to right the plane before they slammed into the ground at six hundred miles per hour. He would have to hope that Boeing built a sturdy airframe.

He grabbed the yoke and pulled backwards. The yoke resisted for a half-second, then gave.

The ground began to tilt even as it rushed them. The nose was raising, but God, it was moving so slowly.

Finally, he saw the horizon. He kept the yoke pulled back, and just before the nose tilted upward, he saw three people on the roof of an office building staring at the plane, hypnotized with shock and fear. They missed the top of the building by maybe fifty feet.

He pulled back until the plane was at about twenty degrees of climb. He had read somewhere that jetliners typically climbed at seventeen degrees, so this was a close enough estimate considering the large margin of error built into those policies.

Then again, the plane had undergone significant stress. He looked for the backup pitch indicator and pushed the nose forward until it showed fifteen degrees.

Then he sighed and slumped to his knees.

A horrible, shearing noise twisted his stomach, followed by a lurch. The plane tilted to the left, and he quickly grabbed the yoke and straightened it.

He heard a gurgling laugh and turned to see Yusef staring at him, a smile on his face. Blood poured from his mouth, but he laughed again. Alex followed his arm and saw him clutching the lever for the landing gear. That shearing noise was the gear being torn from the plane, and the lurch occurred when the nosewheel impacted the underside of the fuselage before falling to the ground.

Yusef laughed a final time. Then his eyes glazed, and he fell to the deck.

CHAPTER EIGHTEEN

A wave of dizziness overcame Alex. He staggered backwards and fell against the door, gasping and struggling to stay awake. His good hand shook, and when he looked down, he could see blood continue to trickle from the wound in his side.

He needed to bind that wound quickly, or he would bleed to death.

The cockpit had a first aid kit, he knew, but this was beyond a first aid kit. He needed to close the wound fast. "Come on, Alex," he said, "Come on. You can do this."

Outside of the cockpit door, Mahmoud banged and shouted in Farsi. "You're going to have to give me a minute," Alex said, his voice slurring.

He giggled but forced himself to focus. The lightheadedness was due to blood loss, and if he didn't control it, he would lose consciousness. If he lost consciousness now, he would never regain it.

He grimaced and forced himself to his knees. The knife had slid forward now that the plane was climbing and now rested against Bashir's body. He grabbed it and then grabbed one of the dropped machine pistols. He ejected the magazine and pried one of the bullets out.

He had never actually done this before. He knew how it was done, but it was a piss poor way to fix a wound and usually led to life-threatening infection in the future.

Well, he would deal with that problem later.

He pried the bullet out of the casing and lifted up his shirt. He started to pour the gunpowder over the wound, but there was too much blood. It wouldn't light if he did that.

He set the bullet down carefully so it wouldn't spill, then grabbed Bashir's shirt. "Sorry to add insult to injury, buddy."

He dried the blood as much as he could, then reached for the bullet. He could feel his heart pounding. His ears pulsed, and his vision faded in and out. He had seconds left.

He poured the powder over the wound and held his knife over the wound. This would be the hardest part. He wasn't sure if this would actually work, but he had no other choice.

His right hand flopped uselessly over the gun, but that just wouldn't do. "Come on," he growled. "Grab that piece of shit. I don't want to hear any excuses."

He shouted with effort but managed to grip the gun and lift it over his wound. His whole body shook, but he managed to strike the knife on the gun barrel. The first spark missed and seared a black spot onto his skin. The second spark hit the deck harmlessly.

"Come on."

The third spark hit the gunpowder. It went off in a puff of smoke, and Alex screamed as the wound literally melted closed. Dizziness washed over him again, and he fell back against the door, dropping the knife and the gun.

"Air Marshal!" Mahmoud shouted. "You will kill us all! Stop this! Level the plane and come out of here, or I will make you watch me kill the passengers first!"

Alex staggered to his feet. He leaned against the wall and took several deep breaths, allowing his faculties to return to him. He was still in terrible shape, but he had bought himself a few more hours. That would have to be enough.

He pulled himself to the front of the plane and pushed the yoke down. The plane leveled out, and when it was roughly level, Alex looked for the trim tab. That would keep the airplane flying level, automatically making whatever minor adjustments were necessary. Without electronics, it wouldn't be perfect, but Alex had a passing familiarity with how aircraft worked from his time in the military, and a passing familiarity with how airliners worked from his time with the Air Marshal Service. He set the trim to three degrees nose up. Typically, would maintain level flight. Whether that was still the case after the damage the airplane had taken, he didn't know, but they were at fourteen thousand feet now, so they would have a large margin of error and one that would be easily corrected.

When the airplane was level, Mahmoud called to him, trying to sound angry but only sounding relieved. "Now surrender, infidel!"

Alex picked up one of the machine pistols and shambled to the door. "Okay. I'm coming out."

He shuffled toward the door and steadied himself. He leaned against the right wall, holding the pistol in his left, and used his left leg to push the handle down and open the door. Mahmoud instantly threw the door open.

His eyes widened when he saw Alex holding the gun. "Shi—"

Alex tapped the trigger, and four rounds shattered Mahmoud's skull. A bullet flew just past him, grazing his cheek and splintering the windshield. Alex looked through the door to see Hasam adjusting his aim.

Alex didn't need to adjust his.

When the last of the terrorists fell, a wave of relief coursed through Alex. He sank to his knees, and Emma's voice cried, "Alex!"

She rushed forward and dropped to the ground beside him. "You did it! You saved us!"

She pulled away, and her relief turned to horror when she saw his wounds. "Oh God! You're hurt. You're…" Her voice trailed off as she surveyed the carnage in the cockpit. "Holy shit."

"Get on the intercom," Alex said. "Tell the passengers and crew that the terrorists are no longer in control of the plane. Tell them that we're going to arrange for a safe landing somewhere we can be picked up by friendly forces."

She nodded and he said in a quieter voice. "Listen. We have no landing gear. We're going to have to ditch in the Persian Gulf." Emma paled, and he quickly reassured her. "We'll be fine. These airplanes won't sink right away. They're designed to handle emergency water landings."

That was a bit of a stretch and far more than a bit of a stretch considering that there was surely a significant amount of damage to the hull and the wings from having the landing gear ripped off at four hundred knots, but if a water landing was dangerous, a ditch on land would be unsurvivable.

Emma nodded again and composed herself. "Can you fly this plane?"

"I have to."

Emma didn't look entirely reassured, but that was all right. Neither was he.

"You'll be okay?" she asked.

"I have to."

She chuckled, and Alex joined her, both of them laughing at the absurdity of the moment and of their own reactions. "Okay," she said. "You do that."

She stood and walked to the intercom. "Ladies and gentlemen, the plane is no longer in control of the terrorists. The Air Marshal on board this flight is in control."

A cheer carried through to the cockpit, and Emma allowed it for a moment before saying, "You've all endured a lot, and I know I'm asking for more right now, but it's critical that you all maintain your seats until the plane is on the ground. Air Marshal Hawkins is arranging for friendly forces to meet us at a destination far from where the terrorists intended to take us. We're going to be okay, but please hang in there a little while longer."

While she spoke, Alex got to his feet and unstrapped the relief pilot from the cockpit. He felt a pang of guilt when he realized he couldn't remember the man's name. He thought back to the briefing Sarah had given him, and the name came to him. Robert. Robert Durst. And the relief copilot was Isla Montgomery.

"Robert and Isla," he said. "I'm so sorry."

He gently pulled Robert's body out of the way and laid him to rest in the relief cabin. Emma closed her eyes and looked away, her lip trembling.

Alex returned to the cockpit and sat in the pilot's chair. He found the button for the comms and engaged them again.

"TSA New York. Is this Alex or someone else?"

Sarah was doing an admirable job of holding it together, but Alex could hear the tremble in her voice.

"It's Alex."

"Oh, thank God!" she exclaimed. "Alex, are you all right?"

"I'm hanging in there," he said. "Not too bad at the moment. Just been stabbed and shot and beat up a bit. Nothing I'm not used to."

"Your plane almost crashed. You came within two hundred feet of the ground."

"Yes, I know. I was there."

"Stop being an asshole! Is everything okay?"

"Okay is a relative term, but I'm in control of the aircraft. The terrorists are dead, and we're no longer on course to Iran."

"Technically, you are just a different part of Iran."

"Now it's *your* turn to stop being an asshole."

"Fair enough. What's the aircraft's status?"

"The terrorist leader decided to leave us a present before he died. He lowered our landing gear at four hundred knots and all three gears sheared off the airplane."

"Jesus."

"I think he might be on vacation. Jokes aside, we need to make a water landing. It would be great if there were rescue boats waiting for us in the water."

"I can arrange that. You're about two hours from the Gulf at your present heading. Let me reach out to the Navy and see if they can meet you there, or if they need you to move."

"Anything from the Iranian government?"

"The usual bullshit about what they'll do to us if we fly over their airspace or land in their territorial waters. They're still denying everything, of course."

"Well, they'll get to keep doing it, I guess, now that their boys are dead."

"What about the asset? Have you figured anything out about that?"

Alex frowned. "No idea. He or she or they are probably still alive and onboard this plane. They'll end up getting rescued and sent home and then they'll probably do the smart thing and just find a legal way into Iran."

"Well, the CIA's pretty unhappy about their existence, so just so you know, they might want to interrogate everyone."

"That sounds like a problem we can deal with after we land safely."

"Right. Sorry. For now proceed on your current heading. I'll let you know what next steps are." After a moment, she said, "Hey, can you even fly that thing?"

He gave her the same answer he gave Emma. "I have to."

CHAPTER NINETEEN

"All rise."

Alex remained seated for a moment, not standing until his JAG attorney nudged him. He blinked and stood at attention, ignoring the throbbing pain in his right leg. That pain would go away eventually. The rest of it? Probably not.

First his father. Then Ben. Now his unit. All he had left was his mother, but while she might tell him she didn't blame him for what happened to Ben, he could detect the stiffness in her embrace now, the slight strain that she couldn't quite remove from her smile. Her letters still came, but less often now, and when he called her, the conversation was stilted and perfunctory.

He hadn't told her about this. She had heard the details of the event, but he hadn't told her everything. He hadn't shared that this time, he really did blame himself. This time, he really should have suffered. This time, he shouldn't have walked away unscathed.

But he had.

"After much deliberation and after hearing testimony from all sides, it is the conclusion of this court-martial that Lieutenant Commander Alexander Matthew Hawkins is not accountable for the events of February the First. It is the conclusion of this court-martial that Commander Hawkins executed his duty to the utmost of his ability and that he in fact went above and beyond his duty in his effort to protect his comrades from the fate that befell them.

"So, we find the defendant, Lieutenant Commander Alexander Matthew Hawkins, not guilty of the charge of dereliction of duty. We find the defendant, Lieutenant Commander Alexander Matthew Hawkins, not guilty of the charge of criminal neglect. While the following is not a formal charge, we also find that Commander Hawkins is not guilty of incompetence, nor of poor judgment. This was an accident. Nothing more."

After a brief pause, Admiral Borden continued. "Lieutenant Commander Hawkins is to receive five weeks medical leave on the recommendation of his commanding officer. Upon conclusion of that leave, he will report to the Deployment Office at Naval Station Norfolk to receive new orders."

She turned her eyes to him, and Alex hated the compassion he saw in her gaze. "Commander Hawkins, you have survived an ordeal that no one in the Navy wishes to survive but many must. You are not alone. Please don't feel you need to carry this burden by yourself. There are many resources available to you. Please use them."

Alex managed to say, "Aye, sir," but he didn't believe any of it. Of course, he didn't believe it. He was alone. Truly, utterly, completely alone.

And that was exactly what he deserved.

"Alex?"

Alex stiffened and opened his eyes. He looked to his right to see Emma looking worriedly at him. "Sorry to wake you, um, your partner is on the radio."

"Oh. Sorry, Sarah. I'm here."

"Good. You had me worried for a minute. Are you all right?"

"Again, that's relative, but I'm alive, and the plane is still in my control."

"Good. We're about thirty minutes out from where I want you to touch down, so it's time to begin descending. I'm going to turn you over to Captain Henry Samuelsson. He's going to guide you through the process."

"Thank you, Sarah."

"Don't mention it. Here's Captain Samuelsson."

A moment later, a grandfatherly voice said, "Alex? You there?"

"I'm here, sir."

"No need for dir. Harry is fine. Listen, you're going to be fine, okay? We're going to make this nice and gentle. Slow and steady is the name of the game. You're going to be losing five hundred feet a minute, so you're not making much of an adjustment at all. We'll start by pulling the throttle back to twenty percent power."

"Only twenty?"

"That's all you need. We'll keep an eye on your airspeed but think of it like the transmission in a car. At highway speeds, you're only using about twenty or thirty percent of your power to maintain a high rate of speed. All you're doing now is pulling the throttle back to just before that so you slow gently."

Alex nodded and pulled the throttle levers back. Conveniently, there was a détente marked 20%. Alex reddened a little. Obviously, an experienced airline captain would know what he was doing. Alex didn't need to question him.

"I'll need you to tell me after you follow each of my instructions too, Alex. Your navigation is still cut off."

"Oh, shoot. Actually, I can turn that back on now."

"No, you can't. While you were sleeping, we walked Miss Johnson through the process. Unfortunately, the aircraft's electronics appear to have been damaged, so there's nothing we can do about anything but the satellite radio. I appreciate the thought, though."

Alex chuckled. He knew that Harry's mild attitude was partly a ploy to keep himself calm, but hell, it was working. "No worries. So now that I've got the throttle to twenty percent, what do I do?"

"Take the nose down to three degrees. You can do that with the trim tab, not the yoke. It's a little easier that way."

Alex moved the trim tab to three degrees descent, and the airplane nosed down slightly. The movement was barely perceptible, but combined with the reduced throttle, Alex felt his body lighten, the telltale sign that the craft was descending.

"Perfect. Now what?"

"Now we have a little bit of time before we need to do anything else. The most complicated part of landing is actually adjusting attitude and throttle when lowering the gear and making sure you place the main wheels on the runway at roughly the same time, so believe it or not, this is actually going to be a slightly easier landing than normal. Far more terrifying—no use in pulling your leg there—but easier."

"I'll take it."

"I'll bet. So for the next twenty minutes or so, you're not going to do anything else, but when that time's up, you're going to pull the throttle to idle and extend your flaps to one hundred percent. When your airspeed drops below two hundred knots, you'll pull your nose up to keep lift so that you glide into the water instead of belly flopping. Did they make you belly flop in BUD/s?"

Alex laughed. "No, but we had a sadistic CPO who would make us stand at parade rest and sing the national anthem while he smacked our stomachs with a wet oar."

"Jesus. Glad I went the Air Force route."

"Are you Air Force?"

"Yes, sir. Twenty years flying C-17s and now nine flying Dreamliners. Can't say I've ever ditched one in the water before, though, Globemaster or Dreamliner. I have to say, I'm a little envious."

"Feel free to come take my place," Alex said.

Harry laughed. "If I could take you up on it, I would. Don't let the mild-mannered voice fool you. I was known as Hellraiser Harry during my days in the Air Force."

"I'll bet you had a lot of fun."

"Well… I don't know if fun is the word I'd use, but I was proud."

Alex smiled wistfully. "I know exactly what you mean."

"So while we're waiting to pull the flaps, let's do a little check on you. How are you doing?"

"I'm all right. The rest helped. I'm in pain, but I'm functional. I'll make it long enough to get to help, then the docs can tell me how bad it really is."

"All right. I'm sure you're telling me the truth, and I'm also sure that as a former Navy SEAL, you're significantly tougher than I am. Still, it wouldn't hurt to designate a copilot just in case you need to take a rest."

Just in case I die, you mean.

Alex turned to Emma. "They need a copilot, in case… well, in case."

Emma's face was white as a sheet, but she didn't hesitate. "I'll do it."

Alex smiled and nodded. "I have a volunteer, Harry. Emma—that is, Miss Johnson has agreed."

"Excellent. Go ahead and have her take the copilot's chair now. I'd like her to familiarize herself with the controls."

Alex looked at the copilot seat, still occupied by First Officer Montgomery. "Give me two minutes, Harry."

He took the headset off and got to his feet. Emma looked away while he removed Montgomery from the copilot's chair and set her next to Durst.

The seat was torn and covered in blood, but there wasn't anything he could do about that. "Are you sure you want to do this?" he asked Emma.

Emma took a deep breath and squared her shoulders. "I'm sure."

She sat in the chair, tensing at the feel of the blood and the bullet holes. She shivered once, then took another deep breath and steadied herself. Alex took a moment to admire her, then handed her the headset and sat in his own chair. "Okay, Harry, she's online. Go ahead."

"Miss Johnson? You there?"

"Yes. You can call me Emma."

"Okay, Emma. How are you doing?"

She gave a nervous laugh. "Well, I'm still alive. That counts for something, right?"

"It certainly does. Okay, Emma, if all goes well, you won't be doing anything but sitting in a chair for a few minutes. That being said, it doesn't hurt to be prepared. So, here's what I need from you. You need to know where seven pieces of equipment are. The first is the one you're wearing. That headset is your lifeline. As long as you can hear my voice, you'll survive this, all right?"

"All right."

"Good. The second piece of equipment is the channel tuner for the satellite comms. That should be located at the bottom of a small green screen. It might look grey if the power is cut off to the screens."

Emma looked around, and Alex pointed to the knob Harry was referencing. "Okay, got it."

"Wonderful. The third piece of equipment is the yoke you're holding in your hands. That's how you steer the plane. It's not quite like driving a car, though. Turning the yoke engages the ailerons and banks the wings. Pushing or pulling it engages the elevator and points the nose up or down. Turning the plane involves a combination of both. Hopefully, you won't have to do any of that, but if you do, don't worry. It seems a whole lot more complicated and scary than it actually is."

"Don't worry, not scary. Got it."

"Good. The fourth piece of equipment you need to know are the throttles. There should be two, one for each engine, and they should be in between your seat and Alex's."

She located the throttle and nodded. "Yep. They're at twenty percent right now."

"Good. Number five is the trim tab. Hopefully, you won't have to touch that, but if the plane starts to move unpredictably, I'll help you use the trim tab to fix that. That should be located on the control panel near the yoke. You have one on your yoke as well, but that's only useful for small manual corrections. The one on the control panel is basically a mechanical autopilot."

"Is it the one set to three degrees?"

"Negative three degrees?"

"Oh. Yes,"

"Then yes. Number six is the flaps switch. It should have four positions: Zero, plus five, minus twenty and minus one hundred."

"Yeah, I see it."

"Good. Number seven are the rudder pedals. Your feet are probably resting on them right now. They feel like the gas and brake pedal in a car."

"Yeah, I feel them."

"Okay. We may use those to assist in landing depending on the wind. For now, just know that pushing the right pedal down will turn the airplane right very slowly and pushing the left down will turn it left very slowly. That's not entirely correct, but it's good enough for our purposes."

"Then it's good enough for me."

"Wonderful. I'm going to review what we'll be doing in a few minutes, so you're up to speed in case you need to take over from Alex. Alex, while I'm doing that, do you think you can tell the cabin crew to begin preparing for a water landing?"

"Sure, I can do that."

"Outstanding."

Alex got up and shuffled to the intercom in first class. The passengers gasped when they saw him, and several cried out in horror. He managed a smile, which probably didn't help, and tapped the intercom.

"Okay, folks. This is Federal Air Marshal Alex Hawkins. We are about twelve minutes away from making an emergency water landing in the Persian Gulf."

Several more first class passengers gasped and cried out, and he was sure similar reactions were occurring throughout the plane.

"I understand this may seem frightening, but we are in contact with a twenty-nine-year veteran of large jets with extensive experience in this exact model of aircraft. He's going to guide us safely into the water where we will be picked up by a United States naval vessel or vessels and returned home. What I need from all of the passengers is to remain calm and follow the instructions of your flight attendants. Cabin crew, please prepare for water evacuation. Emma and I will put the plane down, and then we'll follow your instructions and get off of this plane."

He left it at that. There wasn't really anything he could say to make this less frightening for the passengers, and continuing to dwell on the fact would just make them more anxious. Besides, he needed to return to the cockpit and begin the next phase of the descent.

He returned to his seat and put his headset back on. "All right, Harry. Are we ready to put the flaps down?"

"You're about forty-five seconds too early, but that's all right. Go ahead and pull the throttles back to idle, then put the flaps to one hundred percent. Do it in that order. Flaps aren't likely to shear off the way the landing gear did, but let's put as little stress on the wings as possible."

Alex followed his instructions and said, "Okay, what's—"

Emma gasped, and Alex turned to her to see a knife pressed against her throat. He looked behind the chair to see the owner of the knife. This man appeared more unassuming than any of them. He was in his late thirties with a round face and weak chin. His belly stuck out like a basketball, and he was a good ten inches shorter than Alex.

But his eyes held the same professional gaze that Yusef's had right up until the final struggle.

"Turn this plane toward Bandar Abbas," the terrorist said. "Do it now."

CHAPTER TWENTY

Alex stared at him, rage, shock, and a touch of bitter humor warring for supremacy in his mind. There was one more terrorist after all. One more person who… Wait.

"You're the asset. You're the passenger they were ferrying."

"Yes, but they didn't know that. They thought I was a member of their crew. I was that also, but I felt it was best to hide in plain sight, both from the passengers and from the hijackers. That is the only explanation you'll receive, so consider it an honor. Turn the plane toward Bandar Abbas."

"I can't do that. Too many people are at risk."

"This person is at risk now if you don't do it." He yanked Emma's hair back, pressing the knife deeper against her throat. She gasped but kept her composure.

"Alex?" Harry called over the radio. "Alex, what's going on?"

"Hold on, Harry."

He reached for the mic to cut off the connection, but the asset said, "It's fine if he hears. As long as this plane lands in Bandar Abbas, everything will work out well."

"How am I supposed to believe you? Your friends—"

"They were not my friends."

"Don't play semantics. The people hired to transport you murdered some of these passengers and threatened to murder others. Yusef actually tried to crash the plane."

"I believe it was his intention to bluff you. However, it was exceptionally foolish, and I understand why you would be upset with him for it. I am not bluffing. Take this plane to Bandar Abbas, or I will kill her."

"And I will kill you."

"Yes. I am banking on the assumption that you will not allow an innocent to die."

Alex glared at him. A very simple ploy, but a very simple truth. Alex wouldn't allow an innocent person to die when he could act to save them.

He wished desperately that his right hand still worked. If it did, he would disarm this prick and send him to hell to join his friends.

But it didn't work. So, all he could do was try to buy time. He glanced at the clock on the control panel. Eight minutes.

"Listen, how am I supposed to know you'll let everyone go?"

"It doesn't matter. They will be released regardless of whether you believe me or not. But only if I reach Bandar Abbas. If I don't, then all of your lives are forfeit."

"You're that important."

"Yes."

Alex scoffed. "If you were that important, they would have arranged better transportation for you than coach on a discount airline that they had to hijack to get you home."

"I don't feel like wasting time explaining every reason why you are wrong. So I'll just issue one more warning."

"Wait. Look, I can't put two hundred ninety lives in danger for one person. I can take you to Bandar Abbas, but you need to convince me that if I do, the other civilians won't be harmed. It's my job."

"My job is to get to Bandar Abbas. I encourage you not to make that difficult for me. I am leaving you alive because I need you to fly this airplane. However, if you give me trouble, I'll simply kill you and learn how to fly this airplane myself."

"We can help each other," Alex insisted. "All I need from you are assurances."

"My escorts gave you assurances. You ignored them."

"They also repeatedly violated those assurances."

"A good faith agreement must be one where both parties do their part. You didn't do yours. You attacked one of the escorts, repeatedly spoke when asked to remain silent and demanded answers to questions we declined to respond to. Believe me, if we wanted to be vindictive, we could be far worse. Now, once more, turn this plane toward Bandar Abbas, or I will kill her in front of you."

Alex checked the clock again. Five minutes.

"I can't do that. Not without knowing that I'm not getting these people killed."

Irritation flashed across the spy's face. His eyes narrowed, and Alex knew he was considering his options. He was perfect for a spy. People worldwide had the Hollywood image of spies as action heroes. In reality, an astonishingly attractive person with an athletic build and skill with weaponry was a terrible choice for a spy. Most of them looked like average people and worked minor jobs adjacent to powerful people.

Their talent was in knowing how to leverage that adjacency to glean information that other people didn't know how to glean.

Their talent was *not* in bluffing an experienced Air Marshal with a military background who knew as well as the spy did that he wasn't about to get himself killed by murdering a civilian in front of him. This spy was just realizing that truth.

The man sighed. "Fine. The plan was—and still is—to hold you all hostage for a week or so. I was to be pulled from the crowd after saying something defiant. They will fake my execution and then drag my body away. Once away, I wake up and tell them everything I know."

"Which is?"

"Classified. This is not the first time we've done this. We'll consider it a learning experience that it doesn't work as well on Americans as it does on poorer countries. The point is that other than being frightened out of their wits for a few days, no one has anything to worry about. If we terrorize a few hostages, then return them to their country and claim no knowledge of the alleged insurgents who took them, then the worst we'll get is a stern lecture. If we kill several hundred American citizens, we'll at the very least see sanctions. Most likely, we'll see war. Contrary to popular belief, we *do* know that it's a war we can't win."

While he spoke, Alex edged closer to him, moving slowly enough that the spy didn't notice. He turned his seat slightly and pushed forward. When the moment was right, he would lunge for the knife and give Emma a chance to escape.

"So trust me when I say we intend to be smart about this. For obvious reasons, I'd appreciate it if you kept this information to yourself, but don't worry that they're going to kill you. That is hilariously bad business."

Alex launched himself at the spy. The man's eyes widened. In the split second it took Alex to reach Emma, he saw shock, then fear, then anger, then resignation and finally determination cross the man's face.

He sliced with the knife. Alex grabbed his wrist a split second later, and Emma cried out as a half-inch-long cut opened on her neck.

The spy glared and tried to cut her more, but even in a weakened state, Alex was more than a match for him. When he realized that he wasn't going to be able to use the knife, he released it, and with more speed than Alex would have thought possible, he dove for one of the machine guns.

Alex sprinted toward him and tackled him just as he brought the gun up. The spy went down easily, but he jammed the thumb of his other hand into Alex's eye hard.

Alex cried out and flinched backward, and the spy twisted his body, rolling Alex off of him. His vision swam, but he felt the gun slip out of his grasp.

Wonderful. I survive all this, and now this little asshole's going to kill me.

If they didn't crash into the water, first.

He heard a cry and looked up to see Emma wrestling with the spy. The spy looked at her in disbelief as she scratched and punched him, wrestling for the gun with ferocious strength for her size.

He swore in Farsi and shoved her off of him, but by that time, Alex was up. He grabbed the gun and sent a crashing blow into the side of the spy's head. The man fell to the ground in a heap.

"Tie him up," Alex commanded Emma. "Use the ropes they tied me with. They should still be in the relief cabin."

"You're going to keep him alive?"

"Yes. I think the CIA would like to have a conversation with him."

Emma nodded grimly and headed for the ropes. Alex staggered back to the pilot's chair, breathing heavily. His body still hadn't recovered all of the blood volume lost.

He put the headset back on and said, "I'm back, Harry. Sorry about that. Looks like there was one more terrorist trying to make a last stand. We took care of him."

"Jesus Christ. Just in time, too. We're two minutes to touchdown."

"Tell me what to do."

"What's your airspeed?"

"One hundred eighty knots."

"Okay. Pull the nose up. We want to be down to one hundred thirty knots when you hit the water. You're looking about ten knots behind schedule, but if you don't lose speed fast enough, we'll pull the air brakes."

Alex heard a groan behind him and turned. The spy was waking up, but not quickly enough to react to being tied by Emma. She looked at him and gave him a nervous smile. He returned a slightly more relieved one.

"Alex?"

"Yes, sorry. Nose up how much?"

"Just three degrees. We want you to be close to level, but we don't want the nose to hit first and flip you over."

Alex returned the trim tab to three degrees up. "Okay. What now?"

"Now we wait."

Alex looked out the windshield. He realized it had been a while since he had done that.

So, even though he knew it was out there, he was surprised to see the surface of the Persian Gulf less than a thousand feet below the aircraft.

His heart began to pound. The last time he had been in a crash, everyone but he had died. Now, he was about to crash the plane on purpose.

He looked at the rapidly approaching water, and for the first time in ten years, he said a prayer.

"All right, Alex," Harry said. "You're moving a little too fast. There are two buttons next to the flaps that say upper and lower spoilers. Hit both of them."

Alex hit them, and the plane slowed and sank rapidly.

"You're fine, Alex. Hold onto the yoke and keep her level. You're touching down in eight… seven… six... five... four… three… two…"

Alex closed his eyes and braced for the impact.

CHAPTER TWENTY ONE

"What do you think, Hawk? A nice, pretty Japanese girl or three? Maybe a nice hotel room in Tokyo overlooking the bay?"

Alex chuckled. "I think you'll be lucky enough to stay out of jail, Munguia."

"Leave the commander alone," Jackson admonished. "He's still hung up on the gunner girl he left on the Dakota*."*

The team all catcalled and whistled as one. Jackson grinned at Alex, who rolled his eyes and let them have their fun. It had been ten years since he and Hannah had enjoyed their little fling on the Dakota, but they had run into each other the week before during leave and shared a drink to catch up. She was now Operations Officer on the Aspen. She was also married with two kids, and they had shared only a drink.

Not that it mattered to the boys.

"Damn, you probably broke that poor girl, huh Hawk? She knew you back when you were a shaver. Now you're a full-fledged Frogman. Be honest, you ruined her for hubby back home, huh?"

"All right," Alex said. "That's enough, guys."

"Yeah," Jackson scolded. "Don't go making fun of the commander's girlfriend."

Alex laughed. Then he blinked.

When he opened his eyes, the scene changed. It was five days later, and they were in a Sikorsky Blackhawk that was missing the last third of its tail boom.

Munguia was nearly dead. He had caught a piece of shrapnel in his chest from the missile strike and while he was still breathing, his eyes had rolled back in his head and his body was limp.

The others were all right, but when Alex and Jackson looked at each other, Alex could tell that they both knew this was it.

"Brace for impact, boys!" he called. "We're gonna have a fun landing!"

"Hell yeah! Time to play, boys!"

Alex felt a rush of pride in his CPO. Jackson was a true American hero. Alex hoped people would remember him that way.

"One hundred feet!" the pilot called. "Oh fuck, oh fuck, oh fuck, oh fuck, oh FUCK!"

Alex closed his eyes.

And opened them to find himself lying on top of something warm and wet. He tried to turn his head, but the movement sent a wave of nausea through his body. He grimaced and fought back the bile that rose in his throat, then got to his hands and knees.

His hands sank into something that felt like canvas. Had he landed on his pack?

He looked down and saw the name patch. Most of it was covered in blood, but he could clearly read JACK.

His eyes widened in horror. Heart pounding, he lifted his gaze to the figure just above that patch, the figure on which his own head had been resting when he awoke.

He was trained to be able to function regardless of the circumstances. He was trained to operate and complete the mission no matter what he experienced or witnessed.

But when he saw the mangled mess that used to be his CPO's head, Alex screamed.

***

The impact jarred Alex to his core. His teeth rattled, and his eyes bounced in their sockets. The plane screeched and groaned, and water washed over the nose, completely obscuring his vision. The yoke jerked in his hand, and it took all of the remaining strength in his good hand to keep it steady.

He heard screaming behind him and could only hope the passengers weren't panicking enough to make problems. He didn't dare hope for anything else.

Finally, after what seemed like an eternity but was probably only a few seconds, the plane slowed and came to a stop. The water receded, revealing that they had landed almost perfectly level on top of the Persian Gulf and were now floating.

They had done it.

Alex's heart leapt. A smile came to his face, and he whooped a cheer, ecstatic to be alive, ecstatic to not have killed anyone in the process.

"Well done, Alex. Go ahead and get out of there. She'll float for a while, but not a long while."

"Understood. Thank you, sir. I hope to see you in person when I get home."

"I think I can make that happen. Good luck, Alex."

Alex disconnected the headset and made eye contact with a shaken but equally elated Emma. "Good job, Em—"

He was cut off when she threw her arms around his neck and kissed him hard. The kiss was brief, but like the landing, it seemed to Alex to last for an eternity.

When she pulled away, she smiled and said, "Thank you."

"Thank *you*. That almost made all of this worth it."

She giggled and blushed, and the color made her look so damned beautiful he nearly kissed her again.

Then the aircraft groaned, and he remembered that they were sinking. "Go help get the passengers off the plane. I'm going to bring triple-oh-zero with me."

The spy rolled his eyes. To be fair, that was a pretty weak attempt at humor, but he was dealing with severe blood loss and multiple injuries. He'd think of something better when he was healthy.

Emma nodded and rushed toward the cabin to help the others evacuate. Alex could see the flight attendants operating like a well-oiled machine, opening emergency doors and deploying rafts with an efficiency that would have made Old Joe proud.

When was the last time he saw Old Joe? He'd have to make a point to call him when he got home.

He thought of his brother, still suffering alone in Des Moines. He'd have to make a point to call Ben too. Even if he didn't answer.

He grabbed the spy with his good hand and hefted him to his feet. "Walk and make no trouble, or I'll leave you here to drown," he growled at the man.

The spy met his eyes with a sour expression and didn't say anything. Still, he made a good pace toward the raft near first class, and when Alex pushed him down the slide, he didn't make a scene at the bottom.

Alex walked through the aircraft, assisting others as they exited. He saw Emma comforting the little boy, who was terrified and trying to stay on the plane. It probably didn't help that Emma was covered in blood.

Still, the boy actually calmed when Emma took his hand in hers and promised to go with him and his mother together. She made eye contact with him and smiled. He returned the smile and nodded, then watched her jump down the ramp.

The aircraft groaned again, and Alex saw water starting to seep in through the doors. They had maybe a minute or two left.

He helped an elderly couple into the exit, earning a grateful smile from the head flight attendant. Several people were injured, and where he could, Alex assisted them.

The water was pooling quickly now. He estimated maybe another five minutes at most.

A thought occurred to him. He hadn't seen any US naval vessels when he landed. Sarah had said they were supposed to be here.

He looked out of the open door and saw nothing on the horizon. He headed to the other side. Still nothing.

His frown deepened. He could understand how difficult it was to happen to be right next to a jetliner ditching in the water, but they were in the middle of the closest thing to a war zone the US Navy had seen since the first days of the Iraq War. He was certain that with the US aware of the situation, they would be the first ones here, but just in case, he ran for the cockpit and collected the TEC-9s.

"Marshal!" the head flight attendant called. "That's everyone! We have to move!"

"Coming!"

Alex rushed back to her, carrying the weapons, and jumped onto the ramp. It was nearly level with the water now, and he had to scoot along on his backside to reach the raft. As soon as he and the head flight attendant were on the raft, the flight attendant quickly cut the raft away from the plane.

She used the attached oar to push the raft away, and they drifted slowly from the wreck.

Alex thought the passengers might cheer now that they were safe from drowning, but instead, a hushed silence fell over the four rafts. They looked at the airplane as it slowly sank deeper into the water, and Alex could see the same sober look on all of their faces.

In an odd way, the big jetliner looked majestic as it slowly sank under the water. Alex felt as though he were witnessing the funeral of some great creature, finally felled after a heroic battle that had seen it victorious but fatally stricken.

He felt a moment of admiration for the tough bird. It had endured far more than any civilian aircraft was supposed to endure, and it had gotten them safely to the surface.

His right hand hung limp, but he lifted it to his forehead anyway. He held the salute until the plane slipped slowly beneath the waves. That too was almost anticlimactic. There was no splash, no suction whirlpool and no noise. It simply slid underwater and disappeared, carrying with it the bodies of six of the seven terrorists.

That reminded him. He looked at the head flight attendant and asked, "Did we retrieve the bodies?"

She bowed her head and shook it silently. Alex sighed. "That's all right. You did an outstanding job. We didn't lose anyone else. That's what matters."

So the plane also carried the bodies of four innocent passengers, one of whom was brave enough to risk and ultimately give his own life to defend an innocent mother and her child.

He lifted his hand in salute again and felt a pang of guilt. He had never gotten the man's name. A cloud settled over him. At least he knew the names of the SEALs he had lost. Had he grown so cold that the lives of others didn't matter to him anymore?

Quit focusing on the dead, Old Joe's voice echoed in his mind. *Take care of the living. Make it up to them that way.*

Alex nodded and said, "Can you get us close to the other rafts? I need one person on each raft to carry a weapon."

The flight attendant seemed to notice the machine pistols he carried for the first time. She paled and asked, "Isn't the Navy going to come rescue us?"

"They will, but I want to be prepared just in case."

"Just in case what?"

"In case my friends come," the spy said.

"You hush," Alex said.

When he saw the grin the man wore, he frowned.

Then he heard it. The whine of outboard motors approaching. He looked toward the sound, and a thrill of fear ran through him.

A half dozen motorboats were racing their way. They were still too far away to see clearly, but Jake didn't need to be up close to know that they were all filled with armed men.

CHAPTER TWENTY TWO

Alex looked at the flight attendant and said, "We need to get to the other rafts now!"

The woman's face was ashen, but to her credit, she kept calm.

"What's going on?" one of the passengers asked. "Are they here to rescue us?"

"No," Alex said.

The woman's eyes widened. She began to hyperventilate, and when she saw the weapons on the boats, she shrieked.

"Stay calm!" Alex said, using his best command voice. "You panic, you die!"

The passengers looked at him in fright, but the panic that threatened was quelled for the moment.

Alex knew that would end the moment the terrorists opened fire.

The other flight attendants caught on to the situation and helped close the distance between the rafts. When he was close enough to be confident of his aim, he tossed one weapon each to the rafts, then cupped his hands over his mouth and said, "Pick one person to shoot! No arguing over who! One person and go! No time to wait! Do *not* hesitate to fire on the terrorists!"

He looked at the approaching boats. They fanned out, and his heart sank. They had four machine pistols, three of them in the hands of civilians, against a dozen assault rifles.

He would have to get one of those boats. That was the only way they'd have a chance.

He handed his TEC-9 to the surprised flight attendant, then called out. "Everyone lay flat! Lay on top of each other if you have to! Make yourself as small a target as possible!"

That would do little to protect them from assault rifles tearing holes through the inflatable rafts, but it would minimize panic and maybe give his shooters a fighting chance.

He stripped down to his underwear, earning an exclamation from the flight attendant. The terrorists began to shout and fire their weapons just as he dove under the water.

Swimming at this point came as easily as breathing to him. His injured hand was annoying, but that was all it was. He quickly put distance between himself and the raft, swimming about seven feet underwater to both hide his movements and protect himself from the rifle bullets. Several speared the water around him, but none hit him. He swam under one of the boats and caught the edge, kicking his legs to keep them out of reach of the impeller.

Go time.

He pulled himself out of the water and went to work. The surprised terrorist at the rudder tried to turn his rifle to Alex, but Alex caught it and kicked him overboard.

The gunner at the bow swung around, but Alex fired the weapon before the guardsman could aim at him.

The guardsman dropped into the water, and now Alex had a boat.

It hit Alex that these were Revolutionary Guard, not terrorists. This was going to cause a bit of an incident. No doubt, the more extreme elements in both countries would use this to fuel anti-American or anti-Iranian sentiment.

Well, that was what happened when you threatened civilians.

Alex swung the tiller and headed for the nearest boat. He moved in a random, zigzag pattern, adjusting the throttle as well to make it difficult for the guardsmen to fire on him. Bullets flew past him, and one cut a chunk out of the starboard edge of his boat, but none of the bullets hit him.

The terrorist at the bow of the front boat aimed at the raft, but when his tillerman shouted at him, he swung the weapon around toward Alex.

Alex aimed, a harder thing than he imagined with his left hand, and fired.

Left-handed or not, his aim was true. The man fell into the water, and the flight attendant dispatched the tiller man with her machine pistol. The boat narrowly missed the rafts, continuing out into the gulf.

Alex turned his boat and quickly identified another target. The gunner aimed his rifle at Alex, and Alex gunned the throttle. The bullets sprayed harmlessly behind him.

Alex aimed slightly ahead of the path of the boat. His bullets hit their target, and once more, one of the civilians killed the tillerman.

Alex felt a moment of remorse. He was trained and conditioned to kill, and he would feel no guilt ending the lives of people who were trying to kill innocent civilians.

But the civilians would feel remorse. Even if they didn't feel guilt, they would always know that they had taken a human life. That was hard. There was a reason why not everyone could become a soldier. It was an incredibly difficult thing to do to take someone else's life.

But it was the guardsmen or them right now, and to Alex, that was an easy choice. He turned his boat back toward the rafts and surveyed the situation again.

There were three boats left. The tillermen had learned their lesson and were staying out of range of the machine pistols. Unfortunately, that was well within the range of their rifles. One of the gunners aimed and fired, and Alex heard a cry to his left as at least one civilian was shot.

He snarled and aimed his own rifle at the gunner, but just as he fired, a bullet struck his rifle. It was a miracle that it hit the rifle and not him, but it ruined the gun.

He dropped it and grabbed the other gun, but that allowed the guardsmen to launch another salvo at the civilians. The cries behind Alex increased, and he yelled in anger and grief as he aimed the rifle at that gunman and fired.

The gunman saw him coming and ducked just in time. Alex shifted his aim but was forced to duck himself when the gunman from the third boat fired at him.

He looked back at the rafts and saw several bodies floating in the water. More concerningly, one of the rafts had been hit and was now taking on water. His blood froze when he saw Emma in that raft frantically trying to bail the water out with the help of a few others.

Another salvo opened holes in his boat, and he spun around and fired quickly to stop the barrage. The two men on the boat ducked, and the two boats passed each other by inches.

Alex turned toward them and saw the tillerman swerve just in time to avoid a burst from one of the TEC-9s. The gunman nearly fell, then lifted his rifle and shot at the civilian wielding the TEC-9. The man dove to the deck before the bullet could hit him, but Alex knew they wouldn't always be that lucky.

Alex's blood boiled. He turned his boat and headed toward the killer, ignoring the bullet's spraying his way from the other two boats and trusting in his speed and their apparently limited competence in fighting on water to save him.

The gunner saw him coming and quickly lifted his rifle, then thought better of it and hit the deck. The tillerman gunned the motor, but Alex caught him just before the boat leapt ahead. The motorboat sped away for sixty yards before the gunner managed to grab the tiller and turn the boat around. By that time, Alex had driven the other two boats away from the raft.

Still, the civilians were sitting ducks. Alex would eventually get the guardsmen, but there was a risk that more civilians would in the process.

Why were they doing this? They were supposed to take hostages, not kill everyone.

Then he understood. They didn't want to leave any witnesses. This op had gone completely to shit, and though they had no way of knowing for sure, they had decided that the civilians probably knew details of their plan and their spy, and they were cleaning house.

And they would get away with it. With no one here to witness, they would claim that the airplane had sunk with all passengers. Everyone would know they were lying, but there would be no proof.

Damn it, Alex was going to lose the people he was responsible for again.

Can't think like that. Have to try.

He fired another burst. He missed the tillerman but hit the engine. It burst into flame, and the tillerman recoiled and cried out as his boat drifted to a halt.

Alex pulled the trigger and heard a click. His weapon was empty.

He turned the boat toward the other boat and accelerated. The two men on board the boat leveled their weapons, but Alex jumped off the boat just before they fired. As he dove under the water, he caught a glimpse of both men diving overboard just before Alex's boat collided with theirs.

That left one enemy boat and four gunmen. Alex swam behind the two men in the water. He waited as the final boat approached, intending to pick them up. When the boat pulled to a halt in front of them, he leapt out of the water and snapped the neck of the gunmen, clamping his forearm to the side of the man's head in lieu of his right hand.

The guardsmen exclaimed in shock, and Alex dove into the water again. Bullets zipped past him, and one hit his back on the left side, but by that time, Alex was deep enough that it didn't penetrate his skin. He turned around and quickly swam toward the other man in the water, who was now struggling over the side. He caught the man's heels just before the boat took off.

Water sliced at his face, but he brought his legs up to the side of the boat and heaved. With a cry, the guardsman fell into the water with him.

Alex saw the boat sashay as the tillerman struggled to get control after the force of Alex's kick. The man he had pulled into the water lifted his rifle to try to strike Alex with the butt, but Alex slammed his head into the man's nose first.

The man cried out and tried to turn his rifle to shoot at Alex. Alex caught the weapon, but with only one hand, his training advantage was finally neutralized. He struggled mightily with the guardsmen, and when the guardsmen reached for a knife, he was forced to let go of the weapon.

The man cried out in triumph and aimed his rifle at Alex.

Then a burst of gunfire blew out the side of his skull. He dropped his rifle and sank beneath the waves. Alex looked to his left to see Emma staring at him in shock, the TEC-9 in her hands.

He felt a moment of mixed admiration and grief for Emma, then grabbed the rifle and looked around for the last boat. It was moving around to the opposite side, putting the civilians between itself and Alex.

Alex swore and swam hard for Emma's raft. It was still taking on water, but the passengers were managing to keep it from filling. Emma and another passenger pulled him onto the raft, and he got up just in time to see another one of the civilians shot off of the raft ahead of them.

Alex lifted the rifle and fired. The two guardsmen went down but not before killing four more civilians, spraying their weapons in a blind rage.

But it was over. Alex sighed and collapsed to his knees.

"Look!"

Alex followed Emma's cry, and his heart sank. More boats were approaching on the horizon, at least a dozen.

He would fight. He would fight until he was killed or until all of them were dead. But with that many attackers, they would almost certainly lose all of the civilians first.

And once more, he would fail to protect those under his care.

CHAPTER TWENTY THREE

"What do we do?"

Alex looked at Emma and fought to keep the despair out of his face. She was so beautiful, so strong, so perfect. She didn't deserve to die here at the mercy of a terrorist government who saw her as nothing more than an obstacle. None of them did.

He looked back at the charging boats. He had one last trick up his sleeve. It had to work. It probably wouldn't, but it was all he had left.

"Let me handle this."

He dove into the water and swam quickly for the first raft, the one he had left the plane on. He climbed on and pointed his rifle at the spy's head.

"Tell them I'll kill you if they fire another shot," he said. "Tell them you die and your secrets with you."

The man's eyes widened. "They won't listen to you! I'm not that important!"

"You were important enough to make them steal a jetliner. They'll do it."

"No, you don't understand! They can't! If any of you survive, then you can confirm they're involvement. They have to kill all of you to avoid war!"

"Then there's no reason I should keep you alive."

"No! Damn it!" He looked anxiously at the boats and shouted in Farsi.

The boats pulled to a stop, surrounding the civilian rafts. Gunners trained rifles on the terrified civilians.

The gunner on the boat directly in front of them aimed his rifle at Alex's head. Alex remained where he was, his stolen rifle steady.

The gunner spoke in Farsi, and the spy translated. "He says you have to release me, or they'll kill everyone."

"Tell him if one more civilian dies, you die."

The spy repeated the phrase, and the gunner unleashed a torrent of speech. Some of it must have been directed at the spy because he paled further and replied with a whine, prompting another torrent of speech before finally telling Alex. "He says you aren't in control and should listen to him."

"Sounds like he said a lot of other things."

"That is all that matters to you. Listen, these are honest men. If you release me, they'll—"

"I'll save you from making an even bigger fool out of yourself. Here's what's going to happen. They're going to take you and me. I'm going to keep my gun on you the entire time. Eleven of these boats will leave now. As soon as they're out of my sight, you and I will step onto the boat directly in front of me. Then we'll leave. They try to stop me, I kill you. They kill me, my gun goes off and you die. They harm a civilian, you die. Tell them that."

The spy was trembling visibly now, but he relayed Alex's instructions. The gunner looked Alex up and down and chuckled, then spoke.

The spy's voice was hoarse. "He says that if you don't release me, he'll just kill everyone. He hopes not to lose me, but if he does, he does. Please. I promise you—"

Alex wasn't sure if his bluff had failed or succeeded, but he would buy them every second he could before it was too late. "Tell him I'll take that bet."

"No! Please!"

"Tell him or die right now."

The spy's fear turned to anger. "You might as well kill me then! They're not going to release any of you! I told you! What do you think they are? Amateurs?"

Alex nodded. It would be a very small silver lining to what promised to be a very dark cloud, but he would take as many of these bastards with him as he possibly could. If he could, he would take all of them. He might not save anyone, but it would be an eye for an eye.

Then he heard a familiar, beautiful, miraculous sound. The shocked and terrified faces of the guardsmen confirmed the sound, and a grin broke out on his face. "Okay. In that case, tell them that if they don't put their weapons down right now, they'll be shredded by about five thousand twenty-millimeter rounds."

The spy didn't translate that, but that was okay. He didn't need to. The sight of two Viper gunships escorting a Sea Stallion transport helicopter was enough to get the message across.

The guardsmen immediately turned their boats around and fled. The spy watched them with an odd mixture of relief and defeat. Alex pulled the weapon away from his head and grinned at him. "Guess you get to live long enough to meet the CIA after all."

The Viper gunships flew past the civilians and continued steadily after the fleeing Guardsmen. More likely than not, they would escort the boats to just outside of range of the Iranian Air Defense System, then turn around and fly back to their vessel.

Speaking of…

Alex turned around and saw a large flattop vessel on the horizon. It was an *America*-class amphibious assault ship. Alex wasn't sure which vessel was stationed in the region right now, but the presence of that ship meant they had a squadron of F-35s, a squadron of Vipers and about sixteen hundred pissed off Marines ready to make Iran very seriously regret any further mistakes.

Alex imagined Iran would already regret this one. The United States wouldn't go to war over this, but he would guarantee that Iran was going to be heavily sanctioned for their actions today.

The Sea Stallion hovered low over the group and a familiar voice called out over the helicopter's speakers. "Commander Hawkins. Need some help?"

He grinned and saluted the gray-haired man standing just inside the open side panel door of the stallion. Captain Joseph "Old Joe" Lincoln, US Navy (retired) saluted back and said, "I'll take that as a yes."

Two crewmen in the helicopter dropped a ladder down the side of the aircraft. "We can take fifty people on the chopper," Old Joe said. "We have boats coming for the rest."

He pointed toward the ship, and Alex turned to see two LCACs heading toward them. The hovercraft would have more than enough room to ferry the remaining passengers to the ship.

At the last possible second, they had been saved.

***

"So, are you unretired, or did you just hop along for the ride on this one?"

Alex sat in the canteen of the *U.S.S. America* sharing a drink with Old Joe. The last of the passengers had been loaded a few hours ago, and they were now steaming to safety.

Old Joe smiled. "I happened to be on board the America as a guest of Captain Hannah Baker."

"Hannah's here?"

"She is. She'll be over to say hello in a few minutes. She needed to be on the bridge until we knew for sure how Iran was going to respond."

"Does this mean they've decided to exist as a country for a little while longer?"

"Looks that way."

"Good for them."

Old Joe lifted his glass to his lips, and Alex looked over his old mentor. Joe's hair was a little grayer and his brow a little more lined than before, but there wasn't even a hint of softness in his powerful arms and broad shoulders. Hell, he could probably take Alex in a fight in Alex's condition.

"How's your arm?" Old Joe asked.

"Still attached."

Old Joe chuckled. "Good to know. Seriously, though, how is it?"

Alex shrugged. "Well, doc says there's moderate nerve damage to… I think he called it the radial nerve. I don't know. Basically, it'll heal, but it'll take a little while. I'll have to take medical leave for twelve weeks or so."

"Damn. That's a long time."

"Yes, it is."

"What are you going to do?"

Alex thought a moment. The past eighteen hours weren't really the worst of his life, considering what he'd seen in combat, but they had been enough to make him reconsider some things. "I think I might go on a date."

Old Joe stared at him a moment. Then he threw his head back and laughed. "Oh boy," he said, wiping tears from his eyes. "You are something, Alex. That's good, though. Jokes aside, that's good to hear. I always wondered why you of all people refrained from taking advantage of your job to get girls. I can't believe you were hung up on Hannah enough to stay celibate for fifteen years."

"Who's hung up on me?"

Alex turned to see a petite but fit woman with dirty blonde hair and a smile that promised all the best kind of danger walking to the counter. The other sailors in the canteen looked nervously at her before finally deciding they didn't have to stand at attention as long as she wasn't looking directly at them.

Alex smiled. "Hannah. Good to see you."

Hannah grinned and wrapped him in a bear hug, then grinned wider and slapped him on his injured shoulder. Alex chuckled. "Nerve damage. Can't feel a thing."

"Dammit. What about now?" She smacked the bandage covering his injured side, and he grunted and winced. "That's better."

"Still violent, I see."

"Always." She sat on Alex's other side and called for the bartender. The CPO running the canteen didn't look surprised at all to see her here. That didn't surprise Alex. Hannah was the king of officer who liked to be a part of the crew, not above it. Some schools of thought appreciated that quality and others didn't, but it had apparently worked for Hannah. Captain of an *America* class vessel at forty was a hell of an achievement.

"So when do you get your star?" he asked.

"Uh uh. I asked first. Who's hung up on me?"

"No one," Alex insisted. "I told Old Joe I was going on a date when I get home, and he decided it must have something to do with our little fling sixteen years ago."

She raised an eyebrow. "Our little fling?"

He rolled his eyes. "Come on, Hannah. Don't act like you were in love. I was just someone to keep your bunk warm."

"I didn't say I was in love, but hell, I thought I made a little more of an impression on you."

Alex rolled his eyes again and sipped his beer. Hannah laughed and shoved him playfully. "Still cranky, I see."

"I'm sixty years old next month," Old Joe said. "What's your excuse?"

"I have you two as friends."

"Oh, are we friends?" Hannah ribbed. "Is that why you call me all the time?"

He reddened a little and said, "That's something else I'm going to take care of. I'm going to be better at talking to people."

Hannah lifted her eyebrow again. "Wow. You almost die again or something?"

"Well, yes, but that's not why I'm making this commitment. I saw…" He hesitated, not sure how to say it.

Fortunately, he was with people who understood without needing to be told. "I get it," Hannah said softly, "and I'm happy for you. I really hope you follow through on this dating thing. It's the flight attendant, right?"

Alex's eyes widened. "How did you know?"

"Besides the fact that it's obvious?"

"How is it obvious? You haven't seen us together."

"Yeah, but she's been asking me over and over how you are, if you're okay, can she see you, et cetera."

"She did. And she will. I wanted to talk to you first."

His brow furrowed. "Why?"

"I was going to tell you not to be an idiot and fuck things up with her, but it looks like you're already on the same page. So I'll just leave it at don't fuck things up with her, you moron."

He chuckled and said, "I'll do my best."

"What the hell is this 'do my best' shit?" Old Joe interjected. "You join the Air Force when I wasn't looking?"

Alex laughed. "What I meant to say, sir, was that I will succeed effortlessly and will make the Navy and the team proud, sir."

"That's what I thought you said. Christ, the man's a civilian for a few years and now he's soft as a desk jockey."

"Go easy on him," Hannah said. "Remember his feelings."

He sighed and sipped more of his beer, prompting another laugh from his two friends. God, he'd missed this. Sometimes, he wished he'd never left the Navy. Other times, he wondered if joining the Navy was the worst mistake of his life.

Ben's face flashed across his mind. That was something else he'd take care of when he got home.

CHAPTER TWENTY FOUR

Alex stood on the observation deck of the *San Francisco's* island and looked out over the gulf. The sun was setting, and in the distance, Alex could see the lights of the Burj Khalifa just over the horizon. They'd reach Dubai in three hours, and he and the civilians would be escorted off the ship. They would enjoy a complimentary night at the Burj Al-Arab hotel—a five-star resort hotel typically reserved for the use of billionaire's, politicians and movie stars—then they would enjoy a free first-class flight home on board nine different Adventure Airlines flights specially scheduled to return them.

Two hundred seventy-six people would, including himself. Twenty-nine would never make it back home.

He looked out over the deck and wondered how the families would react. Not in the short-term, of course. In the short-term, everyone reacted pretty much the same. Shock, grief, anger, disbelief, usually a combination of all the above.

It was the long-term that he thought about. What would they do when the first flush of emotion faded and they got to the serious work of surviving the rest of their lives without their loved one?

Some of them would recover. They would hold the memory of the one they had lost as a treasured recollection in their mind, and they would move on and build a happy life without them. Others would carry their loved one like a weight on their shoulder. They wouldn't move on so much as move through life, but if they were strong-willed and strong-hearted, they could achieve some measure of happiness.

Some people would never move on. They would either remain stuck in the moment of grief and continue through life as a shell of who they used to be, or they would melt down, fall apart and collapse into a broken and slowly dying husk.

A few might even skip straight to the end and cut the word slowly out.

"Hey, you."

Alex turned and saw Emma walking up to him. She wore a blue nightgown and slippers instead of her flight attendant uniform. The casual dress was just as beautiful as the formal wear.

"Hey. I came to see you, but you were sleeping."

She smiled. "Yeah, I guess after everything, I needed a bit of rest."

"I know what you mean."

"Do you? Have you slept at all?"

"No," he admitted. "But I need a different kind of rest."

"Wallowing in guilt?"

He blinked, surprised both by her shrewd understanding of his mental state and her willingness to get straight to the point. "I wouldn't say that," he demurred. "I know that I did everything I could. I just…"

"You hate that it's not enough."

His lips thinned. He looked out over the ocean and nodded.

She didn't say anything for a while. She just put her hand over his and looked out over the sea with him.

The sun dipped below the horizon. The lights of the tallest building in the world grew steadily brighter. Soon, they were joined by stars, a few at first, then a few more. When the lights of the smaller skyscrapers became visible over the sea, Emma finally spoke again.

"I talked to Riley today."

"Who's Riley?"

"The little boy in 29A. He told me he wants to be an Air Marshal when he grows up."

Alex smiled softly. "He does, huh?"

"He does. He said that when he was scared, he thought of how brave you were and how you were going to protect him and his mommy from the bad guys, and he said he wants to be brave like that. So he would tell himself not to be afraid."

"He's a brave kid."

"He is. But he still screamed."

Alex lifted an eyebrow. Emma met his eyes and continued. "When the terrorists threatened to kill his mother, he still screamed. He still cried. He still buried his face in her shoulder and wished he could just close his eyes and wish everything away."

"Well, yeah. He's what, four?"

"Five. But I get your point. Do you get mine?"

Alex thought a moment, then shook his head. "I don't think so."

"My point is that he did his best. And when he said that he wasn't brave enough because he still cried and he wasn't strong enough because he couldn't fight back when they were pointing guns at his mom, I told him that by listening to his mother and doing what she told him, he was being very brave, and he should be very proud of himself. You really can't ask any more out of a five-year-old than that."

"That's true. And I think I see your point, but I'm not a five-year-old kid. I'm a thirty-nine-year-old Air Marshal with twelve years of experience in the US Navy and nine as a SEAL before the Air Marshal Service."

"You're still one person. And you managed to take that airplane away from terrorists who would certainly have gotten all of us killed. Unless you bought that line about sparing our lives."

He thought a while before saying. "I don't know, to be honest. I think that's the hard part. I don't know if they were telling the truth. On one hand, the Iranian government has no love for America or Americans, and certainly no one in Iran would have shed a tear if they decided to gun us all down. On the other hand, killing a jetliner full of Americans is serious. The U.S. isn't nearly as trigger-happy as we were twenty years ago, but there are some lines you don't cross, and that's one of them. It made sense that they would want to get as many of us home safely as possible. Otherwise, why would the terrorists have fought so hard not to kill us on the plane?"

Emma shrugged. "I can think of a good reason. They weren't safe until they were on the ground in their own country. If they killed off the civilians in the air, they wouldn't be safe anymore. The plan, I think, was to land the plane in Bandar Abbas but tell people that the plane vanished over the Persian Gulf. They break the plane up and tow the pieces out past the surf, then leave them there for people to find and confirm the claim. They retrieve their asset and then eliminate any and all witnesses. But if anything went wrong, having three hundred hostages was their safety net."

Alex's eyes widened. "Damn. That makes a hell of a lot of sense, actually."

She nodded. "That was the only reason to disable tracking. No one was going to shoot the plane down. If the hostages mattered, they would have just landed the plane in Bandar Abbas without taking away all of the electronic aids that make that easy. The U.S., as you pointed out, isn't as trigger-happy as it was twenty years ago. They buzz the jet a few times with some fighter jets, but they don't fire a shot, not at the plane or at any Iranian interception. Then it just becomes a few weeks of negotiation before an under-the-table deal is finalized, money changes hands, and we get sent home. But when they turned satellite tracking off, I knew they were going to kill us."

She looked at him. "The way you see it, you lost twenty-nine people. The way I see it, you saved two hundred seventy-five. Maybe that doesn't make up for everyone you lost, but it's a hell of a lot better than it could have been."

She squeezed his hand. "That's my point. You did as much as a thirty-nine-year-old ex-Navy SEAL could have done. And it's a hell of a lot more than most."

He smiled at her. "Are you doing anything tomorrow morning?"

She blinked. Then she laughed. "What? Wow. We have completely changed the subject."

He shrugged. "I've decided to stop wasting time. So are you?"

She laughed. "No, I have no plans for the morning after a few hours of sleep in a hotel following the most terrifying experience of my life. Are you hoping to change that for me?"

"I am. There's a coffee shop on the ground floor of the hotel that serves espresso that's almost as good as what you get in Italy."

"That good, huh?"

"Hey, that's like saying you drive a car that's almost as fast as a Bugatti."

"I have no idea what a Bugatti is."

He chuckled. "Well, it's damned good coffee, in other words."

"Ah." She looked coyly at him. "Well, I can't miss that, can I?"

"I mean, you could, but you'd never forgive yourself if you did."

She looked him up and down. "No. I don't think I would."

They fell silent a second time. She put his hand back over his, and they watched the city of Dubai slowly approaching as the night both darkened and brightened over the Persian Gulf.

CHAPTER TWENTY FIVE

Alex walked into the hospital room prepared for the worst. And somehow, it was still worse than he expected.

Ben lay on the bed covered with hoses and tubes and wires. His entire body was heavily bandaged, and three of his four limbs were in a cast, as well as his hips. His face—what little of it was visible underneath another set of thick bandages—was swollen and a sickly grayish purple that made him look twenty years older than Alex instead of a year younger. Their father had never looked this bad, even at the end, when his body was more tumor than not.

Alex got to experience the distinct displeasure of looking at his brother and wondering how he had even survived.

"Hey, Ben," he said.

Ben didn't say anything. He was conscious. Alex could tell because his eyes moved to rest on Alex when he walked into the room. But he didn't say anything. Maybe he couldn't.

And neither could Alex. What was there to say? What could possibly make this better?

Rage filled him then, so powerful it felt like a blood vessel had burst in his head. He wished vehemently that the police hadn't already caught the assholes who did this to Ben. If they hadn't, then Alex would have made sure they were never found. Or rather that the pieces were never found.

"I hate you."

The words cut straight through the grief, straight through the rage, straight through the nauseating fear and right to Alex's heart. They seemed to have physical power, the blow knocking him back a step. "What?"

"You heard me. I hate you, you fucking asshole."

Ben's voice was a barely audible croak. His lips moved lazily, slowed by the truly exceptional amount of Fentanyl they were pumping into his body to keep him from going into shock from the pain.

But his eyes blazed clear and bright and as focused as Alex had ever seen them. They were the same eyes that told Alex he would marry

Amanda, the same eyes that told him he would make Hawkins Oil a Fortune 500 company.

Ben had married Amanda despite the fact that at the time he said he would, she was dating the captain of the football team, who in addition to being more attractive than anyone Alex had ever seen was the son of probably the only family in Iowa that was richer than the Hawkins family. He had made Hawkins Oil a Fortune 500 company and built a cushion of around twelve billion dollars from the bottom of that list, and he had done it by the time he was twenty-five, all the while surviving multiple hostile takeover attempts from both within and without the company.

If he said he hated Alex, he meant it.

"I'm sorry," Alex said. God, those words sounded so empty. "If I were here—"

"But you weren't. You weren't here. You were on the opposite side of the planet fighting goatherds for control of their desert."

Alex was stunned into silence again. Ben couldn't possibly feel that way about the war. That wasn't why they were fighting. They were trying to make it so that terrorists couldn't attack the United States again. They were—

"Did you win?"

Alex shook his head. "Umm... I mean, not yet. I mean, yes, but there are insurgents—"

"You should go back then. I'm sure they need you. You wouldn't want to let them down, would you?"

"Ben..."

"Fuck off, Alex."

There was no force behind the words. He said them with as much effort as he might use to say, "I'll take a vanilla soft-serve with chocolate sauce."

But his eyes held that same focus. The same intense stare that Alex himself wore when preparing for combat.

Alex wanted to stay. He wanted to think of something to say to convince Ben that he was truly sorry, that this wasn't his fault, that he would do anything to help him recover, to help him get back what he had lost.

But the words died on his lips. There was nothing he could do. He had failed his brother.

So he turned and walked out of the room.

***

"Earth to Alex. You still here, *mijo?*"

Alex blinked and focused his attention back to his partner. Sarah watched him with a wry smile on her lips. "Or are you too important now with that shiny medal on your chest?"

"What medal?"

"The one the President pinned on your chest when you got back home! What medal do you think?"

"But I'm not wearing that medal right now."

"I thought you always wore medals. That's the military thing, right?"

He chuckled. "I think you're talking about the Purple Heart, and the saying is that the real medal is the scar we leave with."

"I don't know, I feel like you've been ignoring me this whole time. It's starting to make me feel like I don't matter to you anymore."

"Sorry," he said. "Just thinking."

"About that blonde girl from the flight?"

He gave her a half-smile. "Sure. Yeah."

"Emma, right?"

"Yes. Emma."

Sarah grinned and said, "Details."

Alex chuckled. "First of all, we didn't do anything. We just had coffee in Dubai and made plans to go out to dinner tonight. Second, if there are ever details to be had, you will not receive any of them."

"Oh, come on. You're no fun."

"Would you want your boyfriend to share details with his female partner?"

"Hell yeah, if they're good details. And they would be *very* good details."

He rolled his eyes. "Well, I don't think Emma would feel the same way."

"Ask her."

"Now you're just being difficult."

She giggled and said, "Well, I need to be. I don't want you thinking I'm going to be all mushy just because you almost died."

"I would never suspect you of being mushy."

"Good. Glad we got that straight. So for real, though, is this going to be a serious thing, or are you just deciding to break your vow of celibacy?"

"For Christ's sake, Sarah, we're going on our first date."

"Your first date? What was coffee?"

"Coffee was coffee."

She stared frankly at him. "Come on."

"What? Not everyone goes from zero to naked in two seconds. We had coffee. Tonight, we're going to have a dinner date. After that, we'll see."

"Well, does she live nearby, at least?"

"Turns out she does. Newark."

"Jesus. Please rescue her from there as soon as you can."

He laughed. "It's not that bad. New Yorkers only say that because they have to."

"I don't live in New York, and I still hate Newark. Crappy is crappy."

"It's not that bad."

"I mean, maybe compared to some Navy bases you used to live on, but compared to anywhere else in the country, it's a craphole."

"I think you've led a very privileged life, Sarah."

She rolled her eyes. "Whatever. So do you think you'll propose to her in time for you to play Santa Claus at the mall, or what?"

Alex sighed. "You're worse than a mother, you know that?"

"Someone has to be your mother, *mijo*. You still don't know how to take care of yourself."

He sighed again. "This is serious."

"The conversation or the relationship?"

"I hope the relationship will lead to something serious. I like her a lot, and I hope that she and I can be something more than just casual."

He expected Sarah to follow that admission up with a crass comment or joke, but instead, she smiled tenderly at him and laid her hand over his. "That's good, *mijo*. I'm glad. You deserve it." She squeezed his hand harder, and her smile vanished. "Don't fuck this up, Alex. You got me?"

"I got you."

"Good. You have what, twelve weeks off?"

"Yes. Less if I can—"

"Bullshit. You have twelve weeks off. That should be enough time for you to get over your fear, so when you come back, I expect to see a beautiful blonde flight attendant kissing you goodbye after she drops you off."

Alex laughed. "I'll do my—" he stopped, remembering Old Joe's admonition. "I'll make that happen."

"Good. By the way, you're paying for dinner tonight, and I'm ordering the most expensive thing on the menu."

"A double bacon cheeseburger with a large fry?"

"*And* a milkshake. You're spoiling me for scaring me to death."

Alex chuckled. "I'll even buy you an extra milkshake to take home."

"Damn straight. So what happened with the spy?"

Alex chuckled again, but this time not with mirth. "I'll never know."

"What do you mean? They don't need you to testify?"

"Something tells me he'll never stand trial."

"What? But that's bullshit! Almost thirty people died because of him."

Alex held her gaze. "The CIA took him. I don't think he'll ever stand trial."

Her eyes widened. "Oh."

"Yeah. That's the part of democracy they don't tell the public about. My guess is he'll be thoroughly interrogated. Once the CIA is confident he doesn't have anything left to tell anyone, he'll either be sent to whatever they're using instead of Guantanamo Bay these days, or he'll be… disposed of."

She grimaced. "Jesus."

"Like I said, this is the part they don't talk about. Can't say I feel bad for the prick, though. That's what you get for murdering innocent people."

"Yeah, I mean, I don't feel bad for him either, but still… it sucks to know that shit like that still happens."

He nodded. "Well, that's why we're here. To make sure it only happens to terrorists."

"I'll drink to that."

He lifted his glass, and she frowned. "I'm not drinking a damned soda for a toast. Time to go to the restaurant, big man. You're going to buy me the most expensive drink on the menu too."

"May I remind you that the medal didn't come with a bonus?" he said drily.

"You can afford it. Your brother's rich, right?"

He stifled the look that wanted to come to his face when she said that. She didn't react, so he decided he was successful. "Yeah, I suppose you're right."

They headed out, and as Alex followed Sarah to the car, it occurred to him that she was right. He did wear his new medal on his chest even if the circle of gold-plated brass was in a cabinet in his bedroom right now. The scars from this mission would linger with him for the rest of his life.

EPILOGUE

Alex stared at the phone for a long time. It was odd how the most difficult things were almost always the simplest things. It was even more odd how a trained combat veteran who had seen, experienced and done some of the most difficult and debilitating things a human being could see, experience or do could have so much trouble handling a simple phone call.

At the same time, it made perfect sense.

Alex had failed twice in his life. Maybe no one else would call it a failure, but he would. There was nothing he could do about the second failure. In a way that made it easier to deal with. He could carry that burden like a martyr without ever having to try to lift it from his shoulders.

But this failure, the first and most painful, he could do something about. Not much, maybe, and not enough to fix it, but enough, perhaps to move on.

And it terrified the hell out of him.

That's good to hear, Frogman, Old Joe's voice echoed in his conscience. *SEALs love scary shit. Pick up the phone and have yourself some fun.*

"Don't know that I'd call this fun, Old Joe."

But he picked up the phone.

And dialed the number.

The person on the other end of the phone answered on the third ring. "Hello?"

Alex took a deep breath and let it out slowly. "Hello, Ben."

Vin Strong

Vin Strong is the author of the BRIANNA DAGGER spy thriller series, comprising five books (and counting), of the ZACK FORCE thriller series, comprising five books (and counting); and of the ALEX HAWKINS thriller series, comprising five books (and counting).

An avid reader and lifelong fan of the thriller genres, Vin loves to hear from you, so please feel free to visit vinstrongauthor.com to learn more and stay in touch.

BOOKS BY VIN STRONG

ZACK FORCE THRILLER SERIES
PATRIOT FORCE (Book #1)
PATRIOT DOWN (Book #2)
PATRIOT RISING (Book #3)
PATRIOT STRIKE (Book #4)
PATRIOT TARGET (Book #5)

BRIANNA DAGGER THRILLER SERIES
MAZE OF SPIES (Book #1)
MAZE OF TRAITORS (Book #2)
MAZE OF LIES (Book #3)
MAZE OF SHADOWS (Book #4)
MAZE OF SECRETS (Book #5)

ALEX HAWKINS THRILLER SERIES
LONE SURVIVOR (Book #1)
LONE TARGET (Book #2)
LONE WOLF (Book #3)
LONE COMMAND (Book #4)
LONE STRIKE (Book #5)

Made in the USA
Coppell, TX
29 December 2025